JERALINE'S ALLEY

BECCA C. SMITH

Published by Red Frog Publishing a division of Red Frog Media

Visit our website at www.redfrogpublishing.com

First published in 2021

Cover Art and Design by Stephan Fleet

Chapter Heading Art by Phoebe Wood
(IG: @Phoebewoodpaints)

ISBN 9781949877335

Printed in the United States of America

<u>Dedication</u>

This story has lived with me for a very long time and in many variations, so it makes perfect sense that I ended up writing the first draft in twenty-one short days. Sometimes when the story is ready, it's ready. To all the dreamers out there: no matter what your age, never give up. Let your imagination guide you and know that someday your dreams will come true.

And to my husband, Stephan: I love you with all my heart and soul! I'm the luckiest person in the world and I thank my lucky stars every day that I found my soul mate and our life together is one big, magical adventure!

HERMIT, STALKER, OR INSANE?
(Ugh. I know. All of the above.)

The night was perfect.

"You are the most beautiful girl in the world, Jeraline. I can't believe how lucky I am," Josh said to me, his eyes staring into mine with an intensity that always made my toes tingle.

"How lucky *we* are," I answered with a dazzling smile.

The moon was bright and full, towering above us as we danced on the large marble-tiled balcony that extended from the castle's ballroom. Other attendants of the ball danced inside, enjoying a night of magic and festivities. The gowns alone were enough for the eyes to feast on for days. But my gown? It was the most stunning dress of them all. Intricate blue, yellow, red, orange, and white crystal beads swirled on top of black velvet, as if a tiny universe existed in its fabric. The bottom of the dress parachuted out to such a fullness I was surprised Josh could reach me. But when he pulled me close, hands gently touching my waist and the fitted corseted top, I shivered with the sensation of feeling perfectly aligned with everything in existence.

Not to be dramatic.

But it felt pretty dramatic.

And Josh.

Everything about him was a dream, from his tailored tuxedo to his beautiful face, but mostly his eyes captured my heart. Those honest, endearingly sweet eyes pierced through my soul, and I instantly knew how much I loved him, and I hoped my eyes told him the same thing.

Because I did.

I loved Josh.

We danced as if in a fairy tale, with the giant castle looming behind us, silhouetted from the bright moonlight. We had danced so far away from the glass doors of the ballroom, I didn't see anyone else anymore.

It was just the two of us.

Me and him.

Him and me.

I didn't need anything else in the world.

He bent down to my ear, ready to tell me something that I was sure would make my heart beat faster.

"I'm sorry, Jeraline, but I think I'm getting too old to dip you," Josh said.

Huh?

"But you're twenty-two."

The scenery shattered in front of me as I now stood in the living room of the apartment I shared with my grandmother, Anna. She held me and looked as if she was about to dip me, despite her reservations of being seventy years old.

"No, *you're* twenty-two," she replied. "And I don't want *you* dipping *me*, so can we call it a night? My back is right at that point where if I turn the wrong way . . . *crunch*. I don't want another pull. The last one had me out for two weeks. I should do my stretches." Grandma pulled away from me and lifted her left arm, stretching sideways.

I was a far cry from my fantasy: hair tied back, my clothes pretty ordinary (jeans and a sweater), and my face as plain as it got, or at least that was the way I saw it. My grandmother, of course, would disagree (what doting grandma wouldn't?).

"Do you need some ibuprofen?" I asked her.

Grams continued to do her stretches as she nodded a big yes to me. I walked over to the counter, grabbed the bottle of pain relievers, and poured her a glass of water.

She stepped closer and took the cup and pill bottle. "Thanks."

Looking around our apartment, I sighed in contentment. It was cozy and warm and had truly become home to us these last three years. It wasn't big by any means, a little less than seven hundred square feet, but for a two-bedroom it was the perfect fit. The living room and kitchen made up the main space, with three doors on the west wall that led to each of our bedrooms and the bathroom in the middle. Definitely no room for a dining room, but Grandma and I usually ate at the couch watching TV anyway. We did have two cherry-red stools underneath the butcher-block-topped kitchen counter, which had a small lip that served as a bar, but I don't think either one of us had used it once since moving in.

A few pictures of us and my parents hung sporadically

throughout the apartment, and the furniture situation was pretty basic: cushy couch, plushy armchair, dark wooden coffee table, and the aforementioned stools. Simple but effective.

Fairy lights draped two of the walls, which didn't help my overactive imagination any since it always gave me hope that when I opened my bedroom door I'd be stepping into another world.

Grandma had put them up after we moved in here three years ago to cheer me up, right after my parents had been killed.

Their twinkling lights had helped me cope at the time.

At least I had Grams though. I didn't know what I would have done if she hadn't been there for me.

Plopping down on the couch, I accidentally let out a huge sigh. It was about as theatrical as they come, though I hadn't meant it to sound that way.

It drew Grandma's attention instantly. "What's wrong, Jeraline?"

I half laughed. "Nothing. I didn't mean to sigh that loud."

"I feel a little better now. We can finish the dance if you like?" Grams didn't seem like she was buying my *nothing* excuse.

"I'm really okay, and I don't want you pulling anything," I responded.

Sitting down next to me, Grandma paused for a minute as if considering something, then trudged forward with the conversation that always made me cringe. "There are so many apps today for dating. You're not interested?"

"Grandma." I sighed for real this time.

"Dancing with your grandmother at nine o'clock at night isn't exactly what I'd imagine a fun time for most people your age." She eyed me up and down, wheels turning when she asked, "What's wrong? You look nervous."

And there it was.

The crux of my "accidental" dramatic sigh. "Tomorrow at the bookstore we're having an author come in and do a signing. I don't want to mess it up." I smiled at her warmly. "And dancing with you is the highlight of my night."

"I don't want you to miss out on anything. You don't go out much, and you don't have friends like you used to . . . It's been three years since we lost my Hannah and Paul," Grandma said carefully.

She was testing me. Testing to see how I'd react. She was right, but I didn't want to make friends. I didn't want friends. Josh was the only one I had even considered being friends with, but I had barely spoken three words to him since he started working at the bookstore a few months ago. And frankly, that was the way I wanted to keep it. I was too scared to put myself out there. It might be worth it, but it might not, and I didn't want to take the risk. Not yet anyway.

Grandma seemed to sense my reluctance to talk about the subject (possibly because I never wanted to talk about the subject) and said, "Being in a relationship isn't the *meaning of existence*, but I was with your grandpa Ed for thirty years before he passed, and let me tell you, Jeraline . . ." She paused, eyes full of wonder as she continued, "It was magical." Grams gently took my hands in hers. "Your parents may have died before their time, but their love was like a fairy tale too. I want that for you. Or if it's not with a person, then whatever else you're passionate about. Sewing? Fashion? Books? Anything you want. I just want you to do it. What about that school you wanted to apply to? Why don't you do that?"

"Grandma, you know I can't afford that." Cassiopeia Design School. It was my dream. A place I could learn about sewing and fashion, because so far everything I knew about sewing was self-taught. But it cost too much money. Who would pay for the loans after I graduated? It was something that was out of reach.

"We could make it work, if it's what you truly want?" Grandma's eyes sparkled with hope.

My defenses shot up like a steel wall as I resisted the urge to yank my hands away from hers. There were a million reasons why I didn't apply other than money . . . a bunch of other things, just none of them were coming to me right now. I didn't dare tell her about the contest the school was running—the prize being a full scholarship. She'd probably do something insane, like try to get me to enter! The truth was: I wasn't ready. I just wasn't ready. She had struck a nerve, but I didn't lash out. I kept my cool and answered, "Someday, Grandma, when we're better off financially." I hoped she'd stop pushing.

She did.

Grandma took her hands away from mine and lifted them in supplication. "All right. No more lectures. I'm one to talk anyway. My butt has been plastered to this couch for twelve years." She cocked her head to the side, musing, "Is it possible to have watched every show available on streaming?"

My chest relaxed from relief at the change of subject. "If anyone can do it, you can," I teased.

That was my cue to leave. Standing up, I kissed the top of her head. "I'm going to bed. I have to make sure everything is perfect

6

at the store tomorrow. I don't want to give Rachel any reason to fire me." Rachel. My boss. The bane of my existence. Tomorrow was a big day for the store, and I didn't want to mess it up.

"You'll do great." Grandma was already surfing through the TV show menu of one of the streaming networks. She'd officially lost interest in my stress attack concerning tomorrow's big event.

I walked through the door furthest to the right as Grandma landed on some kind of British murder mystery show and pressed play.

My bedroom.

My oasis.

My escape from reality.

A tall bookshelf stretched all the way to the ceiling and greeted me on my left, full of every book I'd ever loved. I had an addiction. I loved books. I loved everything about books. And I worked at a used bookstore, so I could hardly be blamed for the amount of books I owned.

Jumping into new worlds, experiencing things I never would in real life: climbing mountains, flying on a giant eagle's back, having superpowers, defeating pure evil. All of it. Reading made me cry, laugh, seethe with rage, be filled with such happiness that I'd have tears of joy. And if I was being honest, the only friends I had were characters from books. I wasn't ashamed to admit it, but I talked to them on a regular basis. Crazy? Probably. But characters in books were easier to connect with than real people. Real people could let you down. Real people could leave. Real people could die.

But not the people in books. Even if they died in the book, they still lived forever, and those were the kind of friends I needed.

7

Next to my bookshelf was my double door closet that held all my sewing supplies and clothes. On the adjoining wall was a single window that overlooked the building next to ours, which was always a bit awkward. Hundreds of glass gateways into strangers' private lives and vice versa. It was why I had thick curtains *and* shutters. I didn't want anyone spying on me, especially since my bed lay right underneath it.

A small table with my sewing machine on top of it was against the wall facing my closet and bookshelf. Right now, I had a couple sketchbooks opened and lying next to the machine, designs I planned on making. When I wasn't reading, I was sewing. It was the only way I knew how to express myself and bring to life what was inside my head. And now that I saw that dress in my fantasy with Josh tonight, I knew what I needed to sew next.

Sitting down on the plushy office chair, I thumbed through the sketchbook, trying to find a blank page to draw on. Ignoring the flyer I had jammed in there about the Cassiopeia Design School contest, I tried to focus on the dress I had imagined in my fantasy. I passed by some of my favorite drawings of gowns that were currently hanging next to me on the portable clothing rack leaned up against the wall. I needed the space to hang them since my closet held mostly fabric and supplies, and I barely had room for actual clothes.

Once I had a design in my head, my brain wouldn't rest until I completed it. Gowns were my favorite. There was something so magical about a full-length dress, especially one with an enormous train. I didn't know if my gowns were any good, but I hoped someday I could make something that would stun anyone who saw it with its beauty.

Picking up a pencil, I began to draw. Before long, I had a rough sketch of what I had seen in my head. A thrill of excitement shot through me, and my mind was already piecing together the pattern. For some reason, my brain just saw how to make things, and I would make them. I couldn't explain it. It would appear like puzzle pieces floating around in my head, and I somehow knew how to fit them all together.

It felt good.

It felt right.

It felt like destiny.

There went the dramatics again. Maybe I did spend too much time alone?

After I was happy with the sketch, I crawled into bed and reached over to switch off the lamp on my nightstand. I paused when seeing the two framed pictures resting on its surface along with my favorite old beat-up copy of *The Gateway to Winterbrook* right next to them. The book was on its last legs, filled with hundreds of creases, pages on the verge of falling out, but it was loved and it showed. Picking up the book, I thumbed through it, glancing at all my favorite marked quotes.

Satisfied, I put the book down and looked at the first framed picture. It was Josh's Employee of the Month photo. *Yes, I stole it. Sue me. I have a problem.*

As if in answer to my gnawing guilt, the character Olivia from *The Gateway to Winterbrook* materialized next to me, sitting on the bed, her adorable twelve-year-old face already eyeing me in disappointment. "I can't believe you stole that from the store."

I tried to hide the shame on my face, but I could tell it wasn't working, so I reasoned with Olivia. "It's like when you first saw the door that led to Winterbrook in the bookstore. It called to you, and you knew it was yours to open."

Olivia rolled her eyes and shook her head. "You are not comparing stealing an Employee of the Month picture on a wall with how I found a gateway into another world, are you?"

"Maybe."

"You should return it." Olivia gave me side-eye.

I knew she was right, hence why I was imagining her. And admitting that made her disappear entirely.

I was alone once more.

Putting Josh's picture down, I picked up the second photo.

My parents. Hannah and Paul Arnold. Happy on the top of the Empire State Building in mid-dance. Staring into each other's eyes, radiating pure love. As I pictured them dancing, the photo came to life and they waltzed with glee, ending with a kiss.

I missed them so much.

Placing the picture back next to Josh's, I looked up at the ceiling and said, "I hope you're still dancing up there." Tracing my finger over their faces, I sighed. "Good night."

2

GUESS WHO'S GOING TO DIE
OF EMBARRASSMENT?
(Why am I so lame?)

I walked up to The Hidden Corner bookstore trying to push down the rising chug in my stomach. My poor gut took the brunt of all my stress, and I wondered how long it could possibly survive, the amount of times I'd put it through the ringer. I'd be dead by thirty at this rate.

Deep breaths.

I won't screw up and embarrass myself. I won't screw up and get in trouble with Rachel. I won't screw up and look like an idiot in front of Josh. I just won't screw up.

Easy.

Except *not* screwing up wasn't in my nature. Born to be a bumbling disaster, I was like that cartoon character that no matter how everything was perfectly set up for them, they'd somehow find a way to utterly destroy it all by simply existing.

The bookstore always lightened my mood though, no matter how much stress I was under. I had found it right after my parents died and thought it was a sign to work there since its name was *The Hidden Corner* and that was the name of the bookstore in *The Gateway to Winterbrook*, where Olivia found the door to Winterbrook. Though Rachel had vehemently denied she named the store because of the book, it didn't matter to me.

I had found it.

It was fate.

And after their death, I had felt compelled to be there. That compulsion was one of the reasons I'd stayed there for three years despite Rachel not liking me.

The building itself was two stories, the top floor being Rachel's apartment (since she owned the store), but the bottom was pure magic. Set on a corner with double glass doors as the entrance where the two walls met, each wall had its own unique design. One side was a row of five giant, plaster book spines almost eight feet tall with classic book titles: *The Illiad, The Three Musketeers, Pride and Prejudice, Great Expectations,* and *Frankenstein.* And the other side was a beautiful mural filled with every book character imaginable all having a picnic at a park by a lake, which I had thought was a tribute to the Stephen Sondheim musical *Sunday in the Park with George,* but I was quickly corrected by Rachel that both her mural *and* the Sondheim play were inspired by the painting *A Sunday Afternoon on the Island of La Grande Jatte* by Georges Seurat. Regardless of how condescending Rachel was with her explanation, it boiled down to a never-ending spiral of inspiration, which was fine with me.

A long line of customers stood against the wall waiting to get in, and as if I needed another reminder, a banner hung above the double glass doors that read: "Author Z.T. Morgan Book

Signing."

My stomach turned into bubble guts, and I instantly wanted to run, puke, or go to the bathroom. (My brain never could give me that pertinent information until it was usually too late.)

One more deep breath and I calmed myself down enough to reach the front door, pulling out my keys.

The woman who was first in line asked politely, "Is Z.T. already in there? I can't see him through the doors."

She was right. The glass doors had a tint to them that kept anyone from looking in.

I smiled politely as I placed the key into the lock. "Should be. We open in five minutes. I'll let you guys in soon."

Nodding, she turned to her friend with a squeal of excitement.

I was more nervous than excited, but that was because I had the tendency to make an idiot of myself in front of people I admired. Vomiting on my favorite designer came to mind, but I really didn't want to remember that right now.

Turning the key, I let myself inside the store.

Pure magic.

Everywhere there were books of every shape and size. Row upon row of eleven-foot shelves like guardians of literature. The odd shaping of the store's space created nooks and crannies where leather, plushy chairs or bean bags were placed for reading. Random stacks of books lay scattered throughout, giving the space a sense of organized chaos. It was the closest place I'd ever found to utopia, and just like in *The Gateway to Winterbrook*, I hoped I'd find the answers I was looking for in here someday. To be able to live even part of my life inside this magical world was worth every second of Rachel's berating.

"You're late."

Speaking of which.

After locking the door, I turned to my right to see Rachel standing by Z.T. Morgan, who sat behind an antique wooden table with intricate carvings along its thick edging. A few stacks of Z.T.'s books were piled next to him, ready to sell and sign.

"I'm five minutes early," I defended myself lamely.

Rachel turned to Z.T. with a shrug. "See what I have to deal with?" Then she focused back on me. Yay. "I needed you here to set up and make sure Z.T. was taken care of."

"But you never told me to come early," I said quietly, but saying it out loud, I realized I should have thought of that. Why didn't I come early? This was a huge day, and of course things needed to be set up. Z.T. obviously came early, as he should have. The fans came early, as they should have. But me? I came five minutes before opening.

Rachel appeared "over it" as we were about to open. She turned to Z.T. with a smile she'd never given to me. "You have everything you need?"

"Yes. Thank you so much, Rachel," he answered politely. His eyes met mine, and I was relieved that there was genuine kindness there. "I'm sorry. I didn't catch your name?"

I walked over and shook his hand, hoping he didn't detect the slight shake and the wetness from the uncontrollable sweat that seemed to have a life of its own. "Jeraline."

"Pleased to meet you, Jeraline." Z.T.'s face was friendly and round, with not much hair on top, though it made him handsome in an old-guy kind of way. He was in decent shape, though some of that roundness stretched around his belly as well.

14

"You, too," I replied shyly. Meeting successful people always brought out my shy card.

I turned to Rachel. "I'm just going to drop my backpack off in the back room real quick."

Rachel stared at me with so much disappointment I thought I would sink into the floor with shame. Why did I annoy her so much? Being twice my age (though she didn't look it; I'd guess she was in her thirties if I didn't know she was forty-eight), I'd think Rachel would have some kind of motherly affection for someone who'd been working at her store for the last three years. But no. She genuinely disliked me no matter how hard I tried to get on her good side.

"Well, go on. We only have two minutes until opening." Rachel shooed me away.

I hurried away and headed to the back room where the employees hung out and stored their personal items. Making my way through the labyrinth of books gave me the confidence and calmness I needed. I was ready for this. I could do this.

Entering the small space, I tossed my backpack in one of five lockers that lined the wall immediately to the left. A small round table with two fold-out chairs was in the back corner next to an old beat-up refrigerator. Before closing the locker, I took out two brown paper bags from my backpack. One had my lunch, and the other had a meal for Hank, the homeless guy I'd become friends with back by the dumpster outside. I placed them both in the fridge, then shut my locker as I left the room.

Arriving at the front of the store again, I stood behind the register, ready to help customers.

Snapping at me to leave, Rachel ordered, "I want Josh at the register. Customers like him better."

Why did I still work here again? Oh right, books. "Okay," I said and stepped away from the register, reaching for the cart on wheels full of books that needed to be returned to the shelves.

"Put those away later. I need you to help keep the Z.T. fans organized so people can shop as well as get their books signed," Rachel barked, looking at me as if I should be psychic and know all of this already.

I walked over to Rachel, my stomach churning yet again.

"You're not going to vomit, are you? Because if you are, please try to make it to the toilet this time. I know you just think of this as the place you work, but I live upstairs. It's my home, and the last time you puked, it smelled for a week."

Now I really needed to throw up.

"I won't puke. I promise." Probably one I couldn't keep if I was being honest.

"Uh-huh. Try to stay out of the way. I don't want you blowing this. This is our first booking of an author that has a real following. If this goes well, maybe we can attract more writers to come here." Rachel seemed nervous herself.

I tried to reassure her. "I won't. I mean, I will stay out of the way, and I won't blow this."

Rachel placed her hands on her hips, obviously exasperated. "You've been working here three years, and you still act like a new employee. No one is going to attack you. Relax, you make everyone nervous."

I wanted to say *No one is going to attack me except* you, but I kept my mouth shut.

Saved by the love of my life, Josh unlocked the front door

16

and let himself in the store.

He smiled at me, and I nearly choked on my own spit.

I'm a winner.

Rachel's eyes glanced at the empty spot where Josh's Employee of the Month picture used to hang. "I'm so sorry someone stole your picture, Josh. You worked so hard."

She knew.

But I'd never admit it.

"We'll get another one of you up there, I promise. I'm really proud of you." Rachel smiled gently.

One thing I'd noticed in the few months that Josh worked here: Rachel treated him as if he were family. It made me wonder if she had kids. In her late-forties, they'd most likely be grown by now, but maybe she was so mean they hated her, so she had to pretend Josh was her boy because her own kids never wanted to see her again.

Okay. I should stop.

But I wouldn't be surprised.

Josh answered, embarrassed at the attention. "I'm not sure what I've done to deserve the title. I've only been here three months, but I appreciate it."

That was easy: *not* throw up. Or more accurately, not be me. There were only two of us anyway. It wasn't difficult to guess who'd be Employee of the Month. Besides, I didn't want to bring down Rachel's wrath if I told Josh I was pretty sure she made the whole title up for him. I'd been working here three years and saw countless employees come and go, and we'd never, ever had an Employee of the Month award. It started a month after Josh began working here. I couldn't complain though, it was how I

17

got my hands on that beautiful photo.

Because yeah.

Big old loser.

Rachel looked up at the clock. "We ready for this?"

Josh and Z.T. smiled at her, both excited, while I shrugged in terror.

Turning to me, Rachel said, "Open the doors."

Walking to the front entrance, I unlocked the glass doors and pulled them wide open. "Could you guys line up against the wall? It's so people can still get inside the shop."

Thank goodness they all listened to me and very politely backed up against the wall as they entered the store one at a time, approaching Z.T.

I noticed a young girl, who couldn't be more than ten years old, holding a pile of Z.T.'s paperback books. She stood fifth in line and looked about as scared as I would have been at her age (let's be honest, at my age too). Before my brain fully comprehended her obvious fear, she broke for the door in a panic run.

I rushed to her side and stopped her, gently touching her arm, making sure she didn't drop her books. "Hey, don't leave. I can see by your books that you're a big fan of Z.T.'s."

"I'm such an idiot. Everyone here has hardcover books, and all I have are paperbacks. He's going to think I'm stupid. My parents are waiting in the car outside. I'm just going to go." Her head hung low in defeat.

"What's your name?" I asked. It was like staring at a past version of myself. I knew that fear of embarrassment well.

"Sarah," she replied meekly.

"Sarah, he's not going to think you're stupid. He's going to appreciate how amazing you are for coming here and bringing every book he's ever written. Especially . . ." I pointed to the well-used spines of all her books, much like my copy of *The Gateway to Winterbrook*. ". . . When it's obvious you've read them quite a bit."

"Fifteen times each," Sarah confessed.

"See? That's incredible. You're what? Ten? Eleven?"

"Ten," she answered.

"Ten freaking years old and you've read all of Z.T. Morgan's books fifteen times? He'll be so impressed. He'll be the one who's nervous."

Sarah's bunched shoulders un-bunched slightly as she began to relax, and it made me relax in turn.

"You think?" Sarah gently bit her lip.

I nodded. "I know. I just met him a few minutes ago, and he's super easygoing and friendly, like Rosar in his books."

Sarah beamed at my mentioning Rosar. "Will you go with me to meet him?"

"Of course I will." I glanced at the line. "Let's get you back in your old spot. Looks like you're up next."

The man that had stood behind Sarah let her back in with a friendly wave. Sarah immediately froze when she came face-to-face with Z.T. Morgan.

Z.T. eyed her paperback books and raised an eyebrow. "Wow. These are all yours?"

Sarah nodded, unable to speak.

I mouthed to Z.T., "Super nervous."

He got it. Z.T. examined each book and saw the cracks in

19

the spines. "I'm honored that you've loved these books so well."

Sarah stared at Z.T., still rooted in place.

Z.T. tried a different tactic. "Who's your favorite character?"

Sarah took a moment, looking up at me for help. I nodded encouragingly and hoped she'd find her voice.

Finally, Sarah turned to Z.T., hands shaking. "Chantrel."

Z.T. clapped his hands together with joy. "I knew it! You remind me of her. I bet you wish you could fly too."

Sarah's shoulders relaxed even more, and she nodded. "I really like that she's smarter than all the boys the most though."

"Just wait until the next book. You're never going to believe what she does to Thrent."

Sarah had completely forgotten about me and was having the time of her life. It filled me with a surging happiness to see Sarah talking to her hero without doing something I would do, like puke or knock over all his books. Small favors.

I moved back to the register, giving them space.

Josh's voice surprised me from behind when he said, "That was sweet of you."

I was way worse than Sarah. I'd been working with Josh for three months, and I still had barely spoken to him. I desperately wanted to say thank you, but my mouth stopped working.

So I did something even better. I laughed in a short, strange huff.

Because that wasn't weird at all.

Thankfully, a customer handed me a book to be purchased right after that beauty of a laugh. My hands shook, but I took the book and rang it up on the register. Apparently, my vocal cords were still on the fritz, so I pointed to the total. When they gave me the proper amount of money, I tossed the book in a bag and handed it back to the customer, wishing they'd stay because now I had to face Josh again.

"What was that all about?" Josh asked innocently.

"What was what? What was what all about?" *Words! I spoke words! It's a miracle.*

"That customer. You looked as though you saw a ghost."

"Oh that . . . that was nothing . . . period I guess."

Okay.

Can I die now?

WHY CAN'T I HAVE NICE THINGS?
(Because those are meant for sane people.)

Yup.

Still here.

Still told the guy I liked that I was having my period.

Okay, time to retreat.

"Excuse me," I said and practically ran into the stacks of the bookstore, not wanting to contemplate the confused expression on Josh's face when I left him.

Why would those words come out of my mouth? Why?

I stopped somewhere in the Classics section, and I verbally grumbled to myself. What now? Should I stand here until . . . what?

Trying to make myself useful (since I was technically at work), I noticed a few books out of place and slid them back into their proper spots.

As I put *The Count of Monte Cristo* back in its rightful home,

Edmond Dantès himself popped into existence next to me. He looked as if he had stepped out of the Château d'If prison, with worn and tattered clothes that matched his worn and tattered skin.

Edmond leaned up against the shelf, shaking his head. "The first time you talk to Josh, and you tell him you're having your period?"

"I got nervous. I don't know. He complimented me. You know I can't handle those. Like at all."

"Clearly. Your imagining me here is proof." Edmond shrugged.

I sighed. "What am I going to do?"

Edmond peeled away from the shelf and stroked his scraggly beard in thought. "A compliment, huh? What did he say? That you're beautiful?" Then he rolled his eyes and said in the most sarcastic tone possible, "What a beast."

I groaned. "No, of course not. He said he thought I was sweet for taking care of that little girl over there."

Edmond peered around the stacks, and his expression softened. "If only you could talk to adults the way you talk to kids and fictional book characters."

"Tell me about it."

Eyeing Rachel near the counter, Edmond's eyes narrowed into slits. "What about that Rachel woman? I have a knack for vengeance. I could help you out?"

"No. I've had enough violence in my life to last a lifetime. I don't want any of that." And if I was being honest, Rachel was the closest thing I had to a mom since my parents were killed. A horribly grumpy, annoying mom, but I'd somehow grown used

23

to her. She was mostly bark anyway, no real bite, so far at least.

"Who said anything about violence? A really good vengeance plan requires taking down a person's internal and external existence. No violence needed." He seemed very pleased by his explanation.

"Rachel is harmless. Honestly, I just think she's miserable and takes it out on me. I don't think she gets out much." As in, not at all. I was pretty sure she never left this building.

"There's no excuse for cruelty. Mean is mean. I don't care what your story is."

"Maybe. But I need this job, so I can handle it." And I loved this job, and I loved this place. I didn't think I could survive mentally without them.

Edmond sighed. "Well, if you need—"

Rachel grabbed my arm and yanked me out of my daydream. "What are you doing back here? I told you to organize the fans!"

"Oh, uh, sorry." I fumbled over my words. Glancing at the doorway, it was crowded with fans, blocking other customers from entering the store.

Before Rachel yelled at me again, I hurried over and said in a loud voice, "Everybody back in single file. We need to clear the door."

I could feel Rachel staring at my back (not really, but the chances were high from the level of anger she exhibited). And since facing Josh was out of the question, I stayed where I was, directing people to Z.T.'s table as they entered the store.

I wished this day would be over already.

***

Surprisingly, I got my wish. The day went fast, probably because of the never-ending line of fans waiting to see Z.T., but even after Z.T. had left, the place stayed busier than normal. That was great for me because I didn't have to talk to Josh or Rachel. I stayed glued to the second cash register or helped customers find the books they were looking for.

And before I knew it, it was closing time. I stood behind the second cash register as Josh and Rachel moved the antique table Z.T. had sat behind, placing it at one of the crannies in the corner where it normally resided for readers.

"That's the last of it," Rachel said as she walked over to the front door and flipped the open sign to closed, then peered over at me. "That went surprisingly well."

I tried to join in on the positive vibe and almost said something back, but I couldn't think of anything, so I stood there, probably giving Rachel a really awkward smile.

She pressed her lips into a line, then added, "No thanks to you."

Josh made one last adjustment to the table, then headed in my direction, ignoring Rachel's comment toward me. "That was fun. Z.T. was super nice."

This appeared to perk Rachel up. "He had nothing but good things to say about you, Josh. You impressed him a lot. Maybe we could get him to read some of your work?"

Josh immediately put his head down and didn't make eye contact with Rachel. The idea of showing his work to anyone, especially an author as established as Z.T., obviously freaked him out. Josh being a writer was one of the things I liked most about him, though I hadn't read anything he wrote. I simply loved that he did. Devouring books was one of my main passions, so it

25

always amazed me when someone came up with stories on their own.

Jumping behind the counter and opening up the main cash register for the nightly count, Josh forced a smile toward Rachel. "That's great. Yeah, maybe."

Awkward.

Rachel didn't seem pleased by Josh's lack of enthusiasm, so naturally she took it out on me. "Take the trash out. I'll count out your register."

And with that, I gladly took my cue to leave. I needed to give Hank his dinner anyway.

After grabbing Hank's bag full of goodies from the fridge, I carried the trash in one hand and his food in the other. Barely able to turn the knob due to both hands being full, I finally moved it enough that I pushed the door open the rest of the way with my hip. Tossing the garbage into the dumpster, I tried not to gag at the smell.

Edmond Dantès leaned against the dumpster, still dressed in raggedy clothing from his Monte Cristo prison. "My offer for vengeance still stands."

Edmond transformed into Hank: the homeless guy I'd become friends with over the years. He had a big grin for me, and I smiled back, handing him the brown paper bag.

"There's a couple of sandwiches and a bottle of water in there. Oh, and my grandma made some peanut butter chocolate chip cookies."

Hank's eyes lit up at the mention of Grandma's cookies, and it made this whole crazy day worth it. "You doing okay, Hank?"

Hank opened the bag and smelled the cookies, his expression

grateful. "I'm better now. Thank you, Jeraline."

"No worries. I'll be closing again tomorrow, so I'll see you then?"

He nodded, and my stomach tightened when his face blushed with shame. I wanted to comfort him and tell him everything was going to be okay, but I knew that wasn't true. I was completely helpless, and the only thing I could do was make sure he was fed whenever I worked a shift.

Although our first encounter had been shaky, we'd gotten to know each other pretty well over the last few years. I can still remember the look of terror in his eyes when he first spoke to me. I had been throwing the wrapper of my breakfast sandwich away in the dumpster, and I heard Hank's voice complimenting my bag. While turning around to face him, I thanked him and told him that I had made it. When we came face-to-face, he must have thought I was startled to see a homeless man standing there, and he had run away, but not before saying he used to be an artist as well. I was horrified that I had caused this sweet old man to run. Fully expecting to lose him, I had to try to get him back, so I called out to him and asked him what kind of artist he was.

And that was the beginning of our friendship. His true passion was painting, but he had never made a living at it, so he worked the odd job here and there until no one wanted to hire him anymore. He had been fifty-eight when he lost his apartment, and he had no family or friends who were willing to take him in. Hank said he'd always been kind of a loner, and it had been the first time in his life that he truly regretted that fact. Thirty years of his paintings were thrown out by the manager of his building. Hank told me he didn't blame the guy, it wasn't as if Hank had a place to store them, but I could tell it hurt him to think about. All that work, passion, and creativity, years and years of it, just gone. All because of money. No money, no life. That was how it seemed to me anyway. He was sixty-one now, and his full social security wouldn't kick in until he was sixty-seven, and I didn't know if he'd make it that long, not without shelter or medical care or . . . human decency.

I wished I were rich so I could rent him an apartment and buy him as many canvases, paints, and paint brushes he wanted. At Hank's age, he should be enjoying the rest of his life, taking vacations, creating all day because he could. I knew he was one of millions, and that only made me angrier about life and how things should be.

My mood now deflated, I mustered up a friendly wave. "Good night, Hank."

"Night, Jeraline. See you tomorrow." He walked away, and I felt slightly better when I heard the crunch of him biting into one of Grandma's delicious cookies.

With one last glance in Hank's direction, I turned and entered the store, locking the door behind me.

I was so close to leaving I could taste it.

Grabbing my backpack from the back room, I tossed it over my shoulder and headed to the front of the store.

Almost out of here.

Rachel finished up the count, and Josh looked ready to go like I was.

I made eye contact with Rachel. "I'm going to head on out, if it's all right?"

So close, only a few steps from the door.

I got the barely-acknowledge-my-existence nod, which sent a thrill of relief through me.

Almost out.

"Good night," I said, taking my key and reaching toward the lock.

"Jeraline, wait," Josh called out to me.

I turned, all fear gone from my body.

"Yes, Josh?"

Josh hurried over to me and held me in his arms. "Jeraline, I can't hide my feelings for you any longer. I love you. I've loved you since the day I first saw you. Say you'll be mine."

We kissed.

Pulling away, I said, "Of course I will."

Yeah.

That didn't happen.

Unlocking the door, I exited into the night air.

Finally out.

Free to go home.

Locking the door behind me, I wondered what Josh must *really* think of me.

Because after today, I'd bet he never wanted to talk to me again.

THE GUN
(Or hand cannon! WTH, Grandma?)

Here it came.

The alley.

I didn't know why I kept walking home this way. I could avoid the alley entirely, but there was something about it, something I needed to conquer. The alley was my enemy. My foe. If I didn't defeat it in some way, my life would be forever ruined. It was as if all the torment in my life had manifested itself into this one alley, the physical embodiment of every fear I'd ever had. And simply walking past it was a test of bravery because I knew if I gave the alley a chance, it would swallow me whole.

The old familiar twist of my gut brought me to reality. Ten feet and I'd be there. My daily fear could almost be construed as "normal" at this point. It certainly happened every time I walked by the alley, *my* alley.

And there it was.

Out of a living nightmare.

Approaching cautiously, I kept at least eight feet of distance from the maw of the beast. Wanted signs plastered the bricked edges, framing the entrance like gatekeepers of evil.

Because that was what this alley was.

Evil.

Evil and alive.

As if all my fears had brought it into existence.

It breathed in and out as I walked by, the darkness within an inky black. I had no way of knowing if someone was standing right there, staring at me as I carefully moved forward. The two side-by-side brick buildings that were forced to share one of their walls with this terrifying dream were affected by the power of the alley as well, their brickwork going from solid red to blackened, moldy stone the closer they were to the entrance. And the sounds! They emanated from the blackness itself, not human, not even animal, though that was the closest reference that came to mind. Growling, snarling, or sometimes a kind of rattling stillness that was scarier than any bestial noise I'd heard.

But today there was a different noise.

The clattering of footsteps.

Someone was in there.

And they were coming out.

I found my feet unable to move.

The silhouette of what looked like a man walked closer, but let's face it, it was probably some kind of demon.

Echoes of gunshots rang in my ear, and all I could think was . . .

Run.

My intuition finally kicked in.

I ran fast, though I knew I must look like a crazy person to anyone who happened to be staring down from their apartment.

I didn't stop until I swung the door open to our apartment building, ran up the stairs, and practically flew into the living room.

I immediately locked the door behind me as if the alley itself had followed me home.

Grandma looked at me from the couch in front of the television, holding her chest from shock. "You scared the crap out of me."

"Sorry. I just got spooked," I admitted without going into detail.

Turning off the TV, Grandma nodded for me to join her. "How was the signing?" she asked.

I plopped down on the armchair next to Grams. "Good. He was super nice, and Rachel was mean, but not the worst."

Grandma grumbled, "There's something wrong with that woman. Do you want me to talk to her?"

"Definitely not. She'd fire me on the spot." I didn't believe that though. Rachel had been horrible since day one, and the puking incident alone should have been means for firing me, but for some reason she kept me around. I was pretty sure in her own warped way she liked me to some degree, but I also wondered if the bookstore itself was watching over me, protecting me in some way. It was like my second home, and even though Rachel was the gatekeeper, I still felt welcome there.

But Grandma seemed to enjoy the idea of me leaving the bookstore. "I'm not sure if that's a bad thing. Ever since your parents were killed . . ." She paused, obviously gauging my reaction, which even I wasn't sure of at the moment. "I haven't seen you do much else but go to work and come back here. You need to get out there, Jeraline."

"Not this again," I groaned. "I'm fine. Really. I like my time at home. I can design and sew and create. It helps me. Honestly."

"What about that boy you have a picture of by your bedside? Josh, is it? You obviously like him."

So embarrassing.

It wasn't as if I hid the picture I stole, but for some reason, having Grams talk about it out loud made me feel like the stalking freak that I was. But my need for advice after today's debacle outweighed my humiliation at the moment. "I get so nervous when I'm around him. I fumble all my words. He probably thinks something's wrong with me."

"I'm sure he doesn't think that. You need more practice talking to people. We need to get you out there," Grandma insisted.

And I wished she'd stop. "What's wrong with me?"

Grandma sat back on the couch and sighed. "Liking someone makes everyone an idiot. Some people are better at hiding their nerves than others is all. I'm pretty terrible at dating too, if you hadn't noticed."

"But you don't want to date." As soon as the words came out of my mouth, I had no idea if it was true or not. I just didn't think of Grams as someone who dated. I figured she was too old to date.

"Who said I didn't want to date? I never did," she answered as if hearing my thoughts. Then she continued, "I'm too damn scared. It's not because I don't want to. And I have a feeling it's the same for you."

I was about to respond when Grandma stood up and went to the counter, grabbing a small cardboard box and bringing it over to me.

It wasn't my birthday or any other holiday or anniversary I could remember. More cookies maybe? But that wouldn't explain the seriousness on Grandma's face.

"I know this might upset you at first, but hear me out," she began.

Uh-oh.

I didn't like the sound of that.

What in the heck was in that brown box?

Grandma sat back down on the couch but close enough to me that our knees touched. She placed the box on my lap. "Open it up."

I was officially freaked.

Slowly, I opened the lid on the box, fully expecting something to jump out and bite me. When the lid opened, I froze.

There had to be some kind of mistake. There was no way in any lifetime that Grandma was giving me a . . .

Gun.

And not just a gun: a very large revolver that looked like it came out of a cartoon western.

Finally, words formed in the back of my throat. "Grandma. What is this?" I said it so quietly I wasn't sure if Grams heard me.

She did.

"I know it's a bit of a shock, but Jeraline, listen to me . . ."

I cut her off and shoved the box back on her lap. "I don't want this! You know what happened to Mom and Dad! They were gunned down! By a . . . *gun!*"

Grandma reached over the box and held my hands in hers. "Which is why I want you to have one yourself. It's registered under your name, but we can return it if you decide not to keep it." She paused, considering the expression on my face, then continued, "Maybe if you felt safe, you'd start living again."

"I am living," I retorted defensively.

Squeezing my hands tighter, she answered, "No. You aren't. You're so scared of life that you're hiding in this apartment."

"I have a job!" Anger seethed through me.

But Grandma stayed calm, her hands tightly grasping mine. "The only reason you keep that job despite that horrible woman is because you're surrounded by books. They've always been your security blankets. You're terrified of losing that job because you'd lose your only other escape." Taking her hands away gently, Grandma placed the open box back on my lap. "We can get you lessons so you know how to use it, so that you feel comfortable with it. Maybe if Hannah and Paul had had a gun that day, things might have turned out differently."

That was it. I didn't want to hear anymore. "Being gunned down with ten other people in a grocery store wouldn't have changed if they had a gun, except maybe more people might have died!"

"You don't know that," Grandma argued.

"You don't know either because it didn't happen. They died. No one else had a gun." I didn't know what I was saying anymore. My insides began to shake having the hand cannon on my lap.

"Will you at least think about it? For me? I'd feel safer if you carried this with you," Grandma pleaded, and there were tears in her eyes. She truly meant it.

I had lost my mother that day, but Grandma had lost her daughter too, and now she seemed convinced that if Mom had carried a gun on her, maybe she wouldn't have died. I understood it, but I didn't know if I could ever agree with it. The weight of the gun inside the box on my lap was enough to make my blood curdle. This was a weapon. A weapon that could *kill* another human being. A weapon that *killed* my parents. How could Grandma ever expect me to be okay with using it?

She begged one more time. "You need to protect yourself."

I repeated the words out loud, "Protect myself."

Protect myself.

Protect myself.

No matter how many times I said it in my head, I couldn't come to terms with the gun staring at me from the box. Guns scared me. Guns terrified me. Guns ruined my life.

But the little voice inside me kept gnawing at me, screaming that I needed to level the battlefield. The bad guys had guns, and unless I planned on making an entire wardrobe made of Kevlar, I'd always be in danger.

I didn't want to live that way though, in constant fear.

But was Grandma right? Was I already living that way? Even without the gun? Would the gun help me feel safe? Would my parents have lived if they had carried a gun? Would they have stopped that murderer from killing all of those people? In this crazy world, did I need a gun? Because if I didn't have one, I'd end up like my parents?

Tears flowed down Grandma's cheeks as she took the box away from me and placed it on the coffee table. "I can't lose you, too," she whispered.

My own tears flooded my eyes before I could stop them. At the same moment, Grandma and I reached for each other, arms wrapping around the only family we had left. I couldn't stop crying, and neither could she. We had mourned for my parents, but it never stopped hurting. The loss never went away, never lessened. It was always there, like a permanent lump in my throat. Maybe having a gun *would* help me stop being scared all the time. Maybe it would give me my power back.

Before I made a decision, Grandma pulled out of the hug and wiped my tears with her thumbs, staring at me with love. "Let's not make any decisions now. Maybe you won't need it. But you and I are going to break out of this self-isolation funk we've put ourselves into regardless."

Um.

Not sure I liked the sound of that either.

At this moment, Grandma was worse than the alley.

"What does that mean?" I asked, afraid to hear the answer.

Wiping away the rest of her own tears, Grandma took a deep breath and smiled (which kind of scared me more). "What do normal seventy-year-olds do for fun?"

"Play weird card games that no one's ever heard of?" I guessed wildly.

"Euchre is fun. I'll get you to like it someday. But no."

"Oh boy. What is it?"

Grandma's smile grew even larger as she said, "We're going to play bingo."

Surprisingly, that didn't sound that bad.

"Okay."

BINGO
(Or as I like to call it: my grandma has more game than me. Yeah.)

Hand in hand, my grandmother and I approached the flashing neon lights beaming the word "Bingo" to everyone in a five-mile radius. Okay, maybe not that far, but it was pretty obnoxious. The letters in the sign had to be at least fifteen feet high. The building itself was an old abandoned warehouse that the local community renovated to be some kind of recreation center, but after a year of almost exclusive bingo playing, they decided to make it a bingo parlor full-time with an occasional rent-out for local events. That had been two years ago. The neon sign was relatively new though, arriving about six months ago. Apparently, the man in charge, Frank Lewis, thought he had bought a much smaller version of the sign, but I was sure he was secretly pleased at the enormous size mix-up.

Older brick apartment buildings surrounded the warehouse, which gave it a homey feel, especially since the renovation design was what Frank called "farmhouse chic." And weirdly, that was accurate. Stained gray wooden siding encompassed the base of the large square building, with red brick filling out the top. The roof was flat, which allowed the neon sign to rest safely, but a nice rustic tin awning covered the ramp and stairs that led to the monstrous sliding barn door that was open at the moment.

This was the first time Grandma and I had ever gone. We'd been hearing about it since it opened, from Grandma's knitting group (which she hardly ever went to; I was starting to see Grandma's point about not getting out), but we kept putting it off, bribing ourselves with sugar and a good TV binge.

Coming here for bingo was a good way for us to turn our "bad influence" on each other into a "good influence" on each other. That was why I didn't argue. Part of me hated going anywhere, but Grandma was right. We *needed* to do this.

Walking through the door opening, we entered a sea of rustic wooden picnic tables and gray hair. There had to be at least a hundred people here, and they were all over the age of sixty. Frank Lewis, the head man himself, stood on a small stage next to a spherical bingo machine cage that blew out numbered balls.

Leaning into the stand-up microphone on the edge of the platform, Frank announced, "B-five."

Maybe this should have just been a "Grandma" outing.

Grandma seemed to come to the same conclusion as she whispered to me, "This probably isn't the best place for a twenty-two-year-old, but at least it gets us out."

"We're definitely out," I agreed as I surveyed the number of wheelchairs and walkers lined against the wall.

And we laughed.

There was plenty of sugar and binge-worthy TV at home if we decided to bail, but for now, Grams said, "We'll play two cards and go. Then we can officially say we went out."

"Deal."

"I'd say let's go now, but I'm trying to be the responsible adult."

"Two cards." I winked.

"Two cards." She winked back.

Near the back, there were two open spots, and we sat down. Every table had a stack of bingo cards lying in the center, so Grandma and I each grabbed one.

A lot of eyes were on me as if they were witnessing a sight they hadn't seen in a while. My trusty stomach already began to turn, but after a few more numbers being called from Frank, everyone re-focused on their bingo cards.

After a while, my mind began to wander, as Frank's voice was strangely soothing, announcing each number. By the time people yelled out that they won, my board was nowhere near any kind of bingo. Before I knew it, my eyes began to droop. Trying to keep my ears out for Frank, I missed a few numbers along the way.

Maybe if I took a little nap sitting up, no one would notice.

"BINGO! BINGO!" A woman in her eighties jumped up and down with glee, waving her arms as if we couldn't all see her.

Clearing his throat, Frank applauded in the woman's direction. "Congratulations, Clarise . . . again."

Ooo. *Again.* Sounded like I missed out on some drama when I spaced out before.

Grandma turned to me, fuming. "This is the second time in a row she's won."

Surprised to see Grandma so angry, I tried to defuse the situation. "She's lucky I guess?"

Shaking her head, Grandma's expression was one of fury. "No. It's fixed."

Time moved slowly as Grandma reached into her purse and pulled out . . .

The gun.

The giant revolver she had given to me before we came here.

But we had left it at home in that cardboard box.

When did Grandma put it in her purse?

And what in the heck was she about to do with it?

Grandma aimed the gun at Clarise.

At Clarise!

The gun!

The crowd audibly gasped at once.

"I'll teach you to cheat!" Grandma yelled as she stood on top of the picnic table.

Blam!

Right in the heart! Clarise went down to a chorus of screams.

"Grandma!"

All eyes turned toward me.

I stood about a foot away from our table, as apparently, I had jumped out of my seat.

Grandma sat at her spot, quietly, no gun, no anger, just utter confusion as to why I had suddenly jumped off the bench and screamed her name in front of a crowd of strangers.

Oops.

Guess I *did* fall asleep.

"Sorry," I apologized to everyone and no one in particular.

41

Quietly, I smooshed back onto the bench next to Grandma, trying not to appear too humiliated, but yeah, pretty embarrassed.

Grandma chuckled as she glanced at me. "Sleepwalking?"

"I may have dozed off." And the two of us were giggling. I didn't dare tell her what I had been dreaming. She'd feel guilty for causing me nightmares by buying the gun. Besides, I still wasn't sure how I felt about the gun yet anyway. The idea of even holding it scared me to bits.

We played a few more bingo cards after that, staying until the place closed down.

As we walked toward the exit with the others, I found myself feeling quite good about our decision to come. "Aside from embarrassing myself completely with falling asleep and scaring everyone, that was fun."

Grandma had a slight pep to her step as she agreed. "I'm glad we decided to stay past the two cards." Then her eyes lit up as she saw something ahead of her.

My curiosity got the best of me. "What's that look about?"

Grandma nodded toward the crowd ahead of us. "You see that guy up there? The one with the flat cap?"

After a moment of inspection, I caught sight of the man she referred to. He was handsome for a guy in his . . . seventies? Eighties? I couldn't really tell. But he carried himself with an air of confidence and charm as he walked with the crowd toward the exit.

"Yeah? What about him?" I had my suspicions on where this conversation was headed.

"His name is Buster, and I met him at the grocery store the other day, but I was too scared to ask for his number. We have a lot of mutual friends, who all tell me he's amazing. They've been trying to set us up for over a year now. It was a total fluke we finally met in the produce section."

The way Grandma stared at the back of his head surprised me, so smitten, so happy, so excited.

"Grandma! Why didn't you tell me? I would've been your wingman. Should we go up to him?" If I couldn't be brave with Josh, I wasn't about to let my grandmother follow in my footsteps.

Grandma appeared shy and a bit frightened. (I knew that feeling well.) "I don't know. Should we? I keep telling you the two of us we need to get out more, but I'm a total hypocrite."

Then it happened.

Buster turned his head as if he had felt our eyes staring at his back, and the most wonderful thing happened.

His face positively beamed when he saw my grandmother.

How could they have just met in a grocery store and look at each other like they were already in love? Anyone could see it. Their eyes sparkled when they made eye contact.

Buster slowed down until we caught up with him. And though we were surrounded by people, it felt like they were the only two in the room. She didn't need me as a wingman. This seemed to be written in the stars.

"Hi, Anna." This confident man was shy in Grandma's presence. "How have you been?" He was too cute.

I hoped I was hiding my oh-my-god-this-is-so-adorable-I-can't-stand-it face well. One thing I knew for sure, Anna Mayberry was definitely my grandmother; her shyness was as painful to watch as mine was to experience.

"Not bad in two days."

Buster relaxed when Grandma spoke, and he began to walk with us. "Has it only been two days? I guess I've been thinking of you a lot. And thinking I should have asked for your number?" He phrased it as a question. (Which was so freaking adorable!)

"I would have loved that," Grandma responded. (Go Grams!)

Buster smiled happily, and I seriously didn't think I could take any more of this adorableness. In fact, I slowed down, unsure if I should leave them alone. At this point, me being a third wheel was an understatement.

Grandma noticed immediately though and, as a parental unit should, pulled me up to her side. "This is my granddaughter, Jeraline."

I had to swoon a little, as Buster's smile was infectious.

He held out his hand for me to shake. "Pleased to meet you. I'm Buster." I shook his hand, then he suddenly looked embarrassed. "But you know that. I'm an idiot." He threw my grandmother another longing look. "I get that way when I'm nervous." Awww.

I really needed to give them some space. "Well, don't be. You two should exchange numbers. I'll meet you outside, Grandma."

"Did you two walk?" Buster asked.

"Yeah, but we don't live far," I said and regretted it as soon as it left my mouth. I'd be willing to bet he was going to offer us a ride, and I ruined it with my stupid politeness.

"Nonsense. I'll give you a ride home."

Phew.

Grandma looked at me with hope, apparently thinking I might refuse. She did hear me when I said I'd be her wingman, didn't she?

"Thank you very much. That's really nice of you," I said, which caused Grandma to beam like human sunshine.

Buster held out his arm, and Grandma took it just like in the movies. My cheeks hurt from grinning at their cuteness as I took a few steps back and watched them talk privately. If I hadn't known they had met only a couple of days ago, I would have thought they'd been together for decades.

A perfect match.

The night air hit my face with a bite of coldness that was glorious. I hadn't realized how stuffy it had been inside the bingo warehouse. The crowd dispersed into cars, loading wheelchairs and walkers inside.

Arriving at Buster's sedan, I sat in the back while Buster opened the passenger door for my grandmother. From the slight crinkle in his eyebrows, I could tell he had been a little disappointed that I hadn't let him open my car door, but I wanted to give them as much time alone as possible.

He started the car, and we were off.

And three minutes later . . .

"Right here will be fine, thanks." I told him it wasn't far.

Buster stopped the car with a small chuckle, realizing how close we had really been. I wanted to give them their "good night" moment, so I exited the car quickly.

Once outside the car, I realized Grandma had the keys.

Yup. I was locked out.

Oh man. I'd have to wait outside the car like a jerk.

Maybe they won't see me, I thought as I shifted closer to the door of our building. But wasn't the rule: if I can see you, you can see me? Because they were parked in front of me as if I were

45

watching a drive-in movie. I wanted to give them privacy, but I also wanted to stare.

My creepy side won out, though to be fair, I only looked out of the side of my eye. It wasn't direct stareage.

Grandma reached over and kissed Buster!

My mouth dropped.

Grams!

Buster turned off the car and exited, hurrying to Grandma's door, opening it for her. Using Buster's hand as support (not that she really needed it), Grandma allowed him to help her out of the car.

Leaning down, Buster kissed her once more, and my own heart skipped a beat at the sight. This was intense.

"Good night, Anna. I'll see you tomorrow night." Buster kissed her one more time.

"I can't wait," Grandma said when they parted.

Buster walked to the driver's side of the car and waved to me. "Night, Jeraline."

"Night." I waved, being the awkward Peeping Tom that I was.

With a honk of his horn, Buster was off and down the street.

NIGHTMARES
(My grandma gave me a gun, what did you expect?)

Grandma hurried over to me with a huge grin.

"Grandma! That was . . . that was amazing!" I was in total awe.

She unlocked the building door, and we walked up the stairs to our apartment. "It felt amazing. I was so nervous and terrified, but I went for it." We entered the apartment, and Grandma turned to me, serious. "Okay. I stepped way out of my comfort zone. Now it's your turn. That boy you have a picture of by your bedside? Your assignment is to have one *real* conversation with him that doesn't involve work. Deal?"

Wait. How did this come around to me? That wasn't fair.

"Grandma, I'm not as brave as you . . ." I practically swallowed my tongue I swallowed so hard.

"Deal?" She had serious-face.

I sighed. "Fine. Deal. But you never said anything about how long the conversation has to be." I had the need to exploit sneaky loopholes at the moment.

"That's fine. Baby steps."

"Kissing a stranger is way bigger than a baby step. You are my hero."

Grandma leaned in to me and gave me a loving squeeze. "I'm old, Jeraline. I have to do everything fast. No one knows how much time we have left. I have to grab it while I can."

"Well, that's both inspiring and depressing. Can we not talk about how much time we have left? Hopefully, I can tap into your bravery tomorrow though, because right now I feel like puking."

Grandma laughed. "You'll be fine. Tomorrow's a big day for both of us. You're talking to a boy you like, and I've got a date."

I leaned down and kissed Grandma on the cheek. "This night has been insane. I'm going to sew a bit to calm my nerves. Is that going to bother you?"

"Never. It makes my heart sing when I hear your machine going. I can't wait to see what you come up with." Grandma picked up the box with the gun in it and handed it to me. "Keep this with you and think about what I said."

I looked down at the box.

I didn't argue.

"Good night, Grandma."

"Good night, Jeraline."

Without another word, I walked into my room, shut the door, and placed the box with the gun under the bed.

Out of sight, out of mind.

I had too many conflicting thoughts racing around my head about the whole topic anyway. I was shocked that I wasn't entirely opposed to the idea. My parents being murdered by a lone gunman kept my brain in full "I hate guns" mode, but I could see the other side of it too when Grandma had looked at me with terrified eyes. Terrified that I could die if I didn't have some kind of weapon to protect me.

Maybe I should learn some kind of martial art instead? Or carry mace in my backpack? Or . . . anything but a gun. I wasn't ready. Not yet.

Walking over to my desk, I sat down in front of the sewing machine and picked up my sketchbook, which was on the page of the dress I had dreamt about. I was pretty sure I had enough of the fabric I wanted, but I needed to check the closet.

Sliding the closet doors open to one side, I took in my floor-to-ceiling shelving unit of uncut fabric, with the middle shelf dedicated to sewing notions. I swear I owned more thread, zippers, snaps, hook-and-eyes, elastic, buttons, latches, clasps, bias tape, and a hundred other things than a fabric store. In fact, I had more fabric than clothes, hence why I had the rolling rack in my bedroom. The amount of space for my everyday clothes in this closet was slim, only taking up about a couple feet of space, but I didn't care.

My wall of fabric was one of my favorite spaces. Staring at the uncut beauties, one word floated in my head: potential. Potential to do or make anything my imagination could come up with. Sewing and creating made me feel alive. It was the only thing I found complete joy in besides reading. It was my own way of creating new worlds and experiencing other people and character's lives and history through clothes. Complete and total immersion. It was so simple. So pure. So beautiful.

And this dress was my next adventure.

I already had an idea of how to make the pattern, and tonight I was going to attempt it, maybe even cut and sew the basic shape.

Skimming through all the fabric, my eyes finally found what I was looking for. It was a fabric I'd had made. There were a few websites that let the customer upload images and designs for their own personalized fabric, and the site I picked also let me pick the fabric type as well. The design I uploaded came from a picture of the universe on the NASA website. I picked it because it contained the image of a star within its swirling galaxy. A very particular star. The star my parents had named after me for my sixteenth birthday. I had pretended to love it at the time, not wanting to hurt their feelings. But at sixteen, I had wanted anything else, not a star I'd never see. So selfish. So materialistic. So stupid.

I had forgotten about it until after they died.

Looking up at the night sky the day after the funeral, I had wondered where they were, if there was such thing as Heaven, or if their souls were free and floating through space. I needed to believe they were around me, watching me, or just near me, and then I remembered the star.

And I knew.

That was where they were.

And they'd be waiting for me someday, forever dancing on the star that was named after their daughter.

It gave me comfort then and still did today.

The website had been running a sale, so I had bought twenty yards of the swirling Milky Way that held the star "Jeraline" in velvet. It was a lighter velvet than the one in my fantasy because I imagined it wouldn't be that easy to print images on classic thick velvet, but this would work perfectly. Being twenty yards, it took up almost an entire shelf, and I was so happy I finally had a project I could use it for. The gown was going to be huge, so I hoped twenty yards would be enough, but I'd make it work.

Leaned up against the wall was a large roll of thin paper that I used for patterns, and a folded up cutting table. Pulling out the table first, I opened its two wings, creating a space of five feet by three feet about waist high. It was a tight fit in my little room, but I'd been sewing for so long I hardly noticed anymore. Lifting the four-foot roll of paper up onto the cutting table, I rolled it out enough to cover the entire surface. Grabbing the cloth tape measure from my notions shelf, I was ready.

Now to put what was in my head onto the paper.

I knew my measurements by heart, so at least that aspect of the process was easy, but I had to think through some of the more difficult sections of the dress, like the top. I wanted it to be the gown version of fit and flare, but I also wanted long sleeves and a half collar that dipped into a V in front. I was reasonably sure I knew how to pattern this, but I wouldn't know until it was made (or sometimes, in the process of being made).

As I sketched out the pattern using my tape measure and my imagination as my guide, my eyes kept veering toward under my bed and what lay beneath. At this point, it was almost like a monster ready to grab my legs if I walked near.

As if hearing my thoughts, Olivia crawled out of *The Gateway to Winterbrook* book by my bedside and sat on the edge of the bed while I worked.

"Thinking about the gun?" she asked.

"You know I am," I answered, trying to focus on my dress

instead.

"Lots of heroes use weapons," Olivia said thoughtfully.

"I'm not a hero."

"Who says? You never know what might happen," Olivia replied quietly.

"Heroes have to be brave, and I'm the furthest thing from that."

"I had to *learn* to be brave. I wasn't at first either. Remember? I may have been looking for a door to another world, but when I found it, it scared the life out of me. I was like you, escaping into books, not accepting my mother's death. If anyone understands you, it's me."

"I'm not like you. I could never be brave enough to do everything you did. You saved Winterbrook. You overcame your grief. You lived a life of adventure. I couldn't do that. I want to. I just don't think I'm capable."

"What you're doing now is a start." Olivia smiled as she examined the sketch of my pattern.

"Making a dress? With nowhere to wear it? That's hardly the stuff of legends." I finished drawing one of the pieces of the bodice.

"You'll find a place to wear it. I have a feeling." Olivia looked like she knew something I didn't. "In the meantime, maybe you should think about what your grandmother said."

"About the gun? I'm too scared to even look at it." Though that part of me was turning into a strange kind of need for it, almost as if I *would* be safe if I carried it with me. Like if I had it in my possession, nothing would ever happen to me. I knew it made no logical sense, but the seed of the idea grew inside of me.

"You should sleep on it. Maybe you'll wake up with an answer," Olivia suggested.

"Maybe," I agreed, but wasn't convinced it would be that easy. "Speaking of which . . ." I looked over at the clock: two a.m. "I have to open in the morning."

Olivia disappeared, and I left everything out as I flipped off the light switch and crawled into bed.

Who knew? Maybe I would have an answer in the morning.

***

I was dreaming.

I stood inside a grocery store, and I knew with certainty that this was *the* grocery store. The grocery store where my parents were murdered.

Customers shopped and walked casually down the aisles.

It was like any other store, nothing unique, nothing special, no reason to fear for your life.

My parents turned down an aisle with their cart, and I wanted to hit pause and stay in this moment of the dream forever, because in this moment they were still alive, but I had no control. I was witnessing their death, and there was nothing I could do about it.

Hannah and Paul Arnold.

My mother and father, who looked almost waxy and cartoon-like as they strolled forward, a cart full of groceries. They laughed and talked without a care in the world. Black mist and mold began to grow on the shelves of food on either side of them like veins pumping in pure darkness.

I wanted to wake up.

53

I didn't want to see what came next.

But I was stuck there, forced to watch their murder. This wasn't the first time, either. I'd seen this hundreds of times in my dreams, in my nightmares.

The blackness spread over people, floors, ceiling, and food as a young man in a mask walked into the grocery store. I knew he was a young man because they had arrested him quickly, and I had memorized every feature of his face, though he hid it now behind his stretch-wool ski mask. He carried a gun, if it could be called that. It looked more like a machine gun or something a sniper out of a movie would carry. An assault rifle, the news had called it. A weapon that killed efficiently and effectively.

The boy didn't say a word. He simply lifted his rifle and began shooting as if he were in some kind of deranged target practice session.

The gunshots were so loud I thought for sure I'd wake up. I hoped I'd wake up. I prayed I'd wake up.

The screams became as loud as the gunfire.

Bodies fell to the floor, disappearing in puffs of black smoke.

My parents had no time to react, to hide, to move . . . anything that might have saved them.

A bullet hit my mother's head, and she died instantly, body falling into my father.

Then three bullets hit Dad's back, and the two of them dropped to the floor, holding each other in death.

The young man walked over to my parents in the aisle. The blackness fully surrounded them, the shelves now molded brick, the ground rotted cement. We stood in the alley. The place where evil lived.

The shooter spit on my parents' corpses, then pulled off his mask.

It wasn't the young man who looked down on my parents.

It was me.

BRING YOUR GUN TO WORK DAY
(Am I really doing this?)

It was morning, and I sat on the edge of my bed. I was still shaken from my dream last night. Seeing my face in the face of my parents' killer wasn't exactly what I'd call a good time. I blamed my grandmother entirely, for giving me the gun.

Space was limited since I left my cutting table out, but I managed to bend down and pull out the dreaded box holding the revolver, without hitting my head on anything.

Lifting the lid, I stared at the weapon for a good five minutes, not sure what I wanted to do.

The dream made me want to both carry the gun with me and throw it into a river at the same time. One well-aimed shot could have saved everyone in that grocery store. Not that I knew how to aim, not that I could have been the one to save them, but still. It had my head racing with possibilities.

Was I really going to carry this thing? Bring it with me

everywhere I went? Bring it to work? I didn't even know how to use it. Grandma was right about that—I'd need lessons. Honestly, I wasn't sure how the thing worked. The only experience I had with the machinations of guns was television and movies, and they just seemed to pull the trigger. And would I be able to do that? Pull the trigger?

I didn't know.

I wasn't ready to think about that.

But I *was* ready to stuff it in my backpack. Okay, not *ready* ready, but I was going to do it all the same. Give it a day. Then I would know how it felt keeping a weapon on me. A gun. How I'd feel having a gun with me during my day. If it drove me to nutzoidville (which I was already thinking it would) then I'd ask Grandma to return it. But . . . if I did decide to keep it, we'd make it official and I'd take lessons.

I sighed in a strange kind of relief.

Deciding to not decide felt good.

Test run.

Yes.

Good.

Okay.

Carefully, I placed the large revolver into the bottom of my backpack and put a cardigan sweater on top for . . . space? Cushioning? Safety? I had no idea, but I decided to wrap it around the gun as if this would somehow stop bullets if I jostled it by accident (knowing full well a flimsy cotton sweater would do absolutely nothing to stop a bullet). Then I put my drawing pad and a few pencils in as well, in case there was some downtime to work on designs. One more thing. I rummaged through the small drawer on my bedside table and grabbed a padlock with a key. If I was going to keep this in a locker at work, I'd need it sealed away. Dropping it into my backpack, I zipped the bag shut.

My stomach began sinking at the thought of having a real conversation with Josh, and strangely, it outweighed the sinking stomach for bringing a gun to work. There was a lot of sinking going on.

Grandma was still asleep, but upon opening the refrigerator, there were two brown paper bags waiting for me. She had placed a note on one that read, "I put in some extra cookies for Hank. Tell him I said hello."

Opening up my backpack again, I put the two bags in there more carefully than I normally would, resting them on top of the cardigan and secretly hoping cookies wouldn't make the gun go off. Irrational, but that was how my brain worked. So far, not looking good for the "keep the gun" argument.

Checking my watch, I noticed I was running a little late, so I hurried out the door and kept a brisk pace heading for the bookstore.

The alley snuck up on me like a second unwanted nightmare. A low, deep chuckle vibrated in my ears as I approached it, laughing at me and my decision to bring the gun with me.

Even in the daylight it was dark and foreboding, mocking me, telling me I wasn't good enough, that I'd always be living in terror, that it would always be here, waiting for me. I wondered if light itself had been sucked into its grasp, like a portal leading to some kind of hell dimension. Holding my backpack closer, as if somehow the gun could protect me through the bag, I ran the rest of the way to work.

I wouldn't let it win.

I wouldn't let it take me.

Running set me free.

Running made me forget.

Catching my breath, I walked into the store to a resounding frown from Rachel (shocker), but I hurried past her and went directly into the back room. I took the two paper bags out of my backpack to put in the fridge, and the gun toppled out of the bag, hitting the floor with a frightening impact.

Boom!

A bullet shot through my gut, blood pouring through the wound. I tried to hold the blood in, but there was no stopping it. I was going to die.

Shaking out of my day-nightmare, I found the gun was safe inside the backpack still covered by my cardigan.

No wounds.

No gunshot.

I needed to stop doing this to myself.

Shoving my backpack into a locker, I locked it with the padlock. No one was getting in there without my key. Tucking the small key into my pocket, I sighed in relief.

Rachel appeared in the doorway, blocking my way out.

"What's in the locker that's got you all worked up?" She eyed me suspiciously.

"My backpack," I answered honestly, but my hands shook.

Rachel walked over and inspected the padlock as if she may find something there.

"I always put it in there," I defended myself lamely.

"Uh-huh." Rachel watched me with mistrust. "You're sweating."

"I ran all the way here, and it's warm back here." All of which was true.

Rachel didn't seem convinced. "Listen, Jeraline, you haven't heard anything about Josh's stolen picture, have you? It couldn't have fallen into your backpack, could it?"

"No." Why wouldn't she let the picture go? *Because you stole it.*

Oh yeah.

"Then why so nervous?" Rachel asked carefully.

Because I have a gun in my backpack. "Too much coffee?" I glanced at the clock on the wall next to us. "I've gotta get out there."

Before Rachel interrogated me more, I skirted around her and walked toward the front counter.

Only one customer was in the store as I reached the main cash register, and he arrived at the counter the same time I did. As the man handed me the book he wanted to purchase, Josh walked in and gave me a little wave.

There went the knees.

I nervously looked away to really cement that I was a jerk in Josh's eyes.

Luckily, he didn't seem to notice as he headed to the back room.

I took the customer's book and saw that it was Jane Austen's *Emma.* One of my favorites. "It's a good one."

The customer handed me the cash. "I have to read it for class, but thanks."

One thing I'd noticed about working in a bookstore: people usually only bought classics for school, that or they were trying to do some sort of reading challenge. Either way, I hoped the guy would enjoy the book.

Josh walked back out until he stood in front of me. *Me.* I didn't think my knees would hold me much longer.

"Hey, I saw you used a padlock on one of the lockers. Would you mind if I put my jacket in there too?" Josh asked politely.

He talked to me.

Did this count as a conversation?

Only if I said something.

I handed him my key and said, "Sure, no problem."

Josh smiled sweetly. "Thanks."

I shockingly smiled in return, silently patting myself on the back as Josh left to the back room once more.

That should totally count as a conversation. Technically we didn't talk about work at all.

Emma Woodhouse from the Jane Austen book *Emma* appeared next to me, dressed in the height of 1800s fashion. Emma glanced in the direction Josh disappeared to. "'Sure, no problem' is not a conversation. You'll have to do better than that."

"Grandma didn't give me any rules except 'no work talk.'"

Emma shook her head, staring at me with disappointment. "Really? This experiment is supposed to help you fall in love."

"I think I prefer liking from afar. Interaction is overrated." These were the commandments I lived by.

Emma shrugged as if I were a lost cause. "Well, if Josh jostles your backpack around too harshly, he may shoot himself by accident and you won't have to worry about having a conversation at all."

Emma disappeared as my stomach dropped and my eyes widened.

Boom!

The sound of my gun was deafening.

Everything moved at a snail's pace.

I ran from the counter toward the back room, but my legs wouldn't move fast enough.

Rachel grabbed my arm, annoyed. "We've got customers, Jeraline."

"I have to pee!" I practically screamed.

Boss lady let me go with a grunt of disgust.

I threw the door open to the back room.

Josh was there, alive, unharmed, no bullets.

But . . . he was about to open the padlock with the key.

"No!" I yelled as if he were about to set off a bomb.

Josh turned to me, shocked and surprised.

I took hold of the padlock and Josh's hand. "Let me, please."

His eyebrows crinkled in outright confusion. I needed a reason. I needed an excuse.

I blurted, "It's just I have some personals in there."

Always with the freaking period. What was wrong with me?

But it worked. Josh's whole demeanor relaxed as he assuredly remembered yesterday's proclamation of my monthly cycle.

"You know what? I'll hang it up in one of the other lockers. I don't need a lock. I think it'll be okay." Josh snapped the padlock closed, and I self-consciously took my hand off of his.

I hadn't even taken a second to acknowledge that we'd been touching that long. I had been so worried about the bag, I barely had time for my belly to do flip-flops from our close proximity. Okay, yup. There were the cartwheels.

He handed me the padlock key. "Thanks anyway."

"You're welcome." Um, what was that? What did that even mean?

Smiling, Josh left, and I hit my head with my fist after he was gone. "You're welcome?"

Emma popped in, leaning against the lockers, smiling. "Now, I don't know about that counting as a conversation, but the hand touching was definite progress."

Rachel peeked in, and Emma disappeared. "Finished?"

I nodded and hurried out to the store, not wanting to face the wrath of Rachel any more than I had to.

Before embarrassing myself any further, I grabbed the wheeled cart full of books next to the counter and pushed it into the stacks to return all the books to their rightful places. After I cleared the first row of returns, there was a tap on my shoulder.

Fully expecting it to be Rachel with some sort of critique on how I was shelving the books wrong, I jumped slightly when it was Josh.

"Sorry," he apologized.

I eyed him nervously. "It's okay. I guess I was just really into this." Good. Words. Progress.

"It's dead in here. Let me help," Josh suggested.

Excuse me? What? Help? Would that require talking? Which I was technically supposed to do with him today, but now that the opportunity was here, all I wanted to do is run. "What about the counter?" Good. Make *him* run, much better.

Josh's demeanor was friendly and carefree. "Rachel's got it."

Oh, good. Now I was stuck with him.

Taking a deep breath, I took a book from the cart and placed it onto the shelf.

So far, so good. I could do this.

Josh grabbed a novel and read the title. "Ooo, *The Gateway to Winterbrook*. I love that movie. It was the only movie my mom bought on iTunes and was pretty much my babysitter most of my childhood."

My fear of Josh vanished as my heart began to race for an entirely different reason. Could it be? Could I finally have found it? Barely able to hide the shake in my voice, I asked, "Is there a gold-leafed door on the opening page?"

Josh opened the book and shook his head. "Nope, just black and white."

Everything deflated.

Fail.

No dice.

I sighed in disappointment. "It was a long shot anyway."

"Something rare?" Josh raised an eyebrow, intrigued.

Nodding, I explained, "The author, Sofia Blackmoor, originally only published three hundred copies in 1907. No one would publish the book because back then publishers didn't think readers would buy fantasy from women, so she published it herself by selling her house. It was picked up later by a pretty big publishing house when they saw how successful she was on her own, but they were too cheap to print the gold inlay. It's like my Holy Grail."

Josh's eyes lit up as he thumbed through the book. "It's crazy that this book almost didn't exist."

"I'd give anything to see that gold leaf page. Some people even say that it's an actual door to Winterbrook." I wanted to gush more, but I restrained myself.

"I never read the book, only saw the movie," Josh admitted. "I should pick this up. You seem to like it a lot, so it has to be good."

I wanted to pinch myself because I was sure I was imagining this wonderful conversation. "The movie didn't do it justice. It left so much of the good stuff out."

Yeah. That was perfect. Insult him. That was better than a pinch.

Josh shifted his feet nervously. His face said it all: he wasn't sure if he had insulted *me* or not, so I tried to fix my blunder by saying, "I love the movie too."

His shoulders relaxed, and he sighed in relief.

I continued, "I just love the book more. My mom used to read it to me every night. I still have a copy too; it's a beat-up mess. She used to say that one day I'd find the first edition. I keep thinking I'll find it here. You see, look . . ." I gently took the book from Josh and opened it to one of the beginning pages. "'Fate had brought Olivia to the front doors of The Hidden Corner bookstore. It had called to her in her dreams, and she knew that everything she had ever wanted was inside its walls.' Still gives me goosebumps."

Josh showed me his arm, and sure enough, he had goosebumps too. "Makes me feel better about working here. You think Rachel named the place because she's a fan of the book?"

"I thought that too when I first started working here, but when I brought up *Gateway to Winterbrook* to ask her, she just got really angry and told me not to talk about 'nonsense books.'" My face burned at the memory. I had hoped it would be a bonding moment, but it was obvious that Rachel had named her store The Hidden Corner for entirely different reasons.

Josh looked back down at the book. "So you think it's your destiny to find the first edition here?"

"That's the dream." And it was. One I wished would come true someday. Maybe the golden page *would* be a door.

Josh glanced at the stacks. "You will. I have a feeling."

Rachel appeared, as if she were a ghost that apparated in front of us. "Josh, I need you at the side entrance to help with some boxes. Jeraline, finish this up later and go to the counter."

"Of course," Josh said, then gave me a small smile and headed toward the side entrance.

And for once, Rachel looked at me as if she wanted to say something more, not in anger, but something thoughtful. She must have decided better of it because she shooed me toward the counter. Viewing the store and its lack of occupants, I decided to go grab my sketch pad before I went to the cash register.

Emma appeared next to the cart and slow-clapped in appreciation. "You did it. A real conversation."

Olivia materialized next to Emma. "You're welcome."

I smiled at that, then feeling pretty good about myself, I placed *The Gateway to Winterbrook* in its slot and headed toward the back room.

TO ENTER OR NOT TO ENTER?
(Why is this such a hard question?)

Carefully unlocking the padlock, I opened my backpack and pulled out my sketchbook, avoiding the sweater-wrapped gun as much as possible.

Zipping up the pack, I shut the locker, secured the padlock, then hurried to the front counter before Rachel discovered that I wasn't there yet.

I made it to the cash registers without incident, placing my sketchbook on the counter and thumbing through its pages. A loose piece of paper fell from the pad and floated to the ground. Picking it up, I examined it closely.

Oh yeah.

Ugh.

The flyer for the Cassiopeia Design School contest.

Emma was back and looking over my shoulder at the rogue piece of paper. "What is that?"

I sighed, staring at the page with longing. "It's an amateur fashion contest. The winner gets a scholarship to Cassiopeia Design School. I really want to go, but we don't have enough money, and I'm too scared to take out loans that I may never be able to pay back," I answered her, not wanting to admit out loud that I was just too scared to enter.

Emma seemed to sense this as she leaned forward. "Jeraline, this is your chance. Your designs are beautiful. Look at that dress there. If I were a bolder woman, I'd wear it myself, and that's saying something considering my impeccable tastes."

"What if they hate them?" I voiced my deepest fear.

"Then they're complete morons, and we'd both know it. You're going to do this. No arguments. You've got to enter soon because the deadline is tomorrow and the pop-up runway is on Thursday." Emma pointed to the printed information on the flyer.

"I waited too long. I can't do this." Why didn't everyone see what *I* did? I wasn't meant to enter.

Emma nodded to the sketchbook full of designs. "You've done the work. You have the time. You haven't missed the deadline. No excuses."

In a huff meant to make her point to me, Emma disappeared. I stared at the flyer.

Could I?

Should I?

But the real question was *would* I?

As Josh headed my way, I hid the flyer and the sketchbook under the counter. He jumped behind the second cash register with a friendly wave. "Not many customers today."

Oh no. Small talk. I was terrible at that. Truthfully, I was terrible at all conversation, but small talk was at the top of the list.

"Yeah." See?

But apparently Josh was determined. "So, what made Jeraline Arnold decide to work at a used bookstore?"

"What made you want to?" Ooo, deflecting. I was good at that.

Josh took it in stride as he laughed. "I'm a writer?"

"You say that like it's a question."

"It kind of is, honestly." Josh sat down on one of the stools behind the counter. "I mean, I love writing. I just don't know if it'll ever be more than a hobby, you know?"

I did. I felt the same way about my designs. "You don't think you're any good?"

"Maybe? I really don't know. I haven't shown anybody. I guess I figure if I don't let anyone read it, I still have a chance. Stupid, right?" He looked at me with a smile, but his eyes darted slightly.

"No. It's not stupid. I'm the same way," I confessed.

"You're a writer?" Josh perked up.

I shook my head, hating to disappoint him. "I sew things." Yeah, that sounded awesome. I explained further, "I want to be a designer."

Josh cocked his head to the side, curious. "Really? You have so much passion for books I thought for sure you'd be a writer or some kind of book critic or something, especially working here for . . . how long?"

"Three years."

"How old are you?" Hearing I worked here three years seemed to pique his interest.

"Twenty-two," I said, marveling at the fact I was functioning in this conversation.

"Me too." Josh leaned back further on the stool so that his back leaned against the counter. "So you've been here since you were nineteen? That's crazy."

"I'm not a writer, but I do love books. Sometimes I think I like books more than I like humans." Oh God. I hoped he didn't think I was talking about him.

But he laughed. "I get that. That's why I started writing. I considered book characters better friends than my real friends, not that I have many of those either."

How was that possible? How could someone so perfect like him not have a ton of friends? Then it hit me. Grandma was going to be so proud of me! This was conversation number two. *Two!*

Oh. I was supposed to respond.

I didn't know what to say.

No.

Awkward silence.

I was ruining the moment.

He said he didn't have many friends, and I was just staring at him.

Help!

Finally, words spilled out of my mouth. "I'm the same way. I talk to book characters all the time like they're real." Literally. Hopefully, he wouldn't think I was a psychopath. "It helps me process . . . stuff." Ah, the elegance.

Josh smiled and stood up from the stool, moving closer to me (well, the main cash register, but for a second I thought he was going to walk right up to me, and my body was on the verge of collapse). "I really love that," he said with such sincerity I was shocked my body *didn't* collapse.

Rachel walked up to us with her usual look of disgust. "Jeraline, you can finish shelving those books now. Josh will stay at the counter with me."

Discreetly, I grabbed my sketchpad and headed toward the abandoned cart amongst the stacks. I didn't look to see if Josh or Rachel had noticed. I hid the pad on the bottom shelf of the cart so I could put it away later. Mindlessly, I began shelving the books back in their rightful places. As I reached the Thriller section, the corner of a piece of paper poked out from under a shelf. Thinking it was garbage, I pulled it out from underneath and saw that it was a photograph. Rachel, at least ten, maybe fifteen years younger, was kissing the cheek of a fourteen-year-old boy. I didn't know what shocked me more: the fact that Rachel seemed so happy and carefree or the fact that the boy looked almost exactly like Josh. The scribbling on the back read: "My beautiful boy Kent."

Kent.

Whoa.

My suspicions had been correct. Rachel had a son. Doing the math from a guesstimation of Rachel's age put Kent around the age of twenty-five? Maybe a little older, maybe a little younger. I wondered where he was. Why he didn't visit. The fact that Rachel had been compelled to hire a look-alike and make him Employee of the Month was both sad and creepy. I wasn't sure how to process it. One thing was for sure though: I didn't want to be caught with this photo. So I did what any normal person would do and stuffed it back under the shelf without a single corner of it poking out.

Filing the picture away as another mystery that was Rachel, I spent the rest of the day shelving the books. Time passed as if I were in some kind of vortex, because it was closing time again.

Grabbing the garbage bag from the back, I opened the fridge, snatched Hank's meal, and left toward the dumpster.

Hank's eyes twinkled as I handed him the paper bag lunch while tossing the garbage inside the metal container. "Hey, Hank."

"Hi, Jeraline. Thank you, and tell your grandmother the cookies were delicious."

"I was hoping you'd say that. She put in a couple extra."

Hank's face lit up, and he tipped an imaginary hat in thanks. "You are too kind to an old man."

"Hey, Hank?"

"Yeah?"

"Do you think you'll ever paint again?" I didn't know why I asked, but I suddenly wanted to know.

His expression turned thoughtful. "I do. Someday."

"I could bring you some supplies: paints, brushes, a canvas? I'd love to see your work." After talking to Josh earlier about what we wanted to do with our lives, seeing Hank made me want to help more. He never saw his dream come true. I knew how much sewing and creating helped me. Maybe it would help him?

But Hank shook his head. "No, Jeraline. I'm not ready for that. I appreciate it though."

"Are you sure?" I desperately wanted him to say yes.

"I'm sure. Besides, where would I put it when it's done?" He cast his eyes down, looking away.

"It would be for me. I'd be giving you the supplies in exchange for a painting for my apartment. Please?" In that moment I'd never wanted anything more.

Hank tilted his head, pondering. "You don't even know if you'd like it."

"If you paint it, I'll like it. Please, Hank? Don't say no." I held my breath as he stood there, thinking.

Finally, he nodded. "Okay. Of course. You've been feeding me for years. I would be honored to paint you something."

Elation flooded through me, and my head was giddy. I hugged Hank tightly.

I nearly choked from the smell, but I couldn't let him hear that. It was so strong that I was afraid my gagging would be involuntary, so I pulled back with a big smile. "Thank you, Hank."

Hank looked positively shocked that I had embraced him. "It's been a long time since anyone has hugged me."

Oof.

My chest ached.

Hank was such a good human who deserved to be hugged daily, but because of something stupid like money, he was here, waiting for a stranger to bring him food.

But I wasn't a stranger.

I was his friend.

"I better get back in. I'll bring the supplies tomorrow. I'm really excited." And I was. I couldn't wait to see what Hank would create.

Hank's head was a little higher, his body a little prouder, and in a confidence that said it all, he replied, "I'm excited too. Thank you, Jeraline." And with that, Hank took out one of Grandma's cookies from the bag and bit down with delight. "These are the best." He walked away with a laugh.

I still smelled a bit of Hank's stench on me, but I figured it would air out as I walked home. Steering clear of Josh or Rachel, I slipped into the back room and unlocked the padlock, taking out my backpack. Cautiously, I surveyed the area once more and then peered inside. The sweater had shifted a bit so the gun's nose peeked out.

Edmond Dantès appeared next to the locker, staring down at the gun. "Honestly, what were you thinking?"

"I have no idea." I really didn't. I had a freaking gun in my backpack, at work. What *had* I been thinking?

"Your grandmother said she'd take you to get lessons. You don't know how to use it. Why wouldn't you wait to learn properly?" Edmond crossed his arms with a grunt.

"I said I don't know!" I snapped. At the imaginary book character from *The Count of Monte Cristo*.

I was seriously losing it.

But Edmond was still there, as real to me as anyone else, as he said, "You could hurt someone, including yourself. This was completely reckless."

"Leave me alone." I shoved the door open and rushed out of the room.

I smelled, I had a gun, I just wanted to go home, take a shower, shove this revolver back under my bed, and never think of it again.

Test day over.

I knew with certainty that I was not a gun person.

Before Rachel stopped me, or worse, made me do something else, I waved to both her and Josh. "Good night! See you guys tomorrow."

Unlocking the door and pushing it open, I didn't hear any arguments.

With one last look to the both of them, I waved slightly, then shut the door, locking it behind me.

All I had to do was get home in one piece.

Easier said than done.

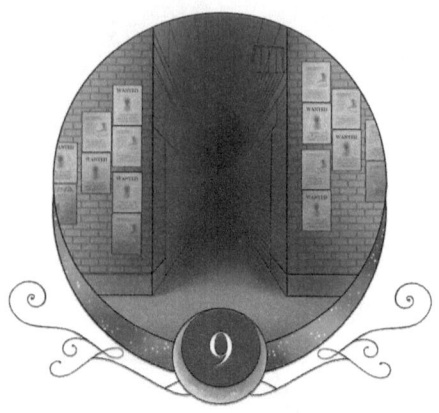

9

THE ALLEY

I sighed in disgust at myself. Racing out of the store wasn't my best move, but I needed to get home.

The bulk of the gun rested against the small of my back from inside the backpack. I couldn't wait to stuff it under my bed and never look at it again.

I tried to comfort myself in the fact that I had two real conversations with Josh today, and I was excited to gush about it to Grandma. It was a big night for her too, and I wondered how her date had gone with Buster. Most likely amazing, considering how they were with each other. It was something out of a fairy-tale book. Love at first sight. My parents always claimed it had been the same for them, and like the sap I was, I believed it. I still believed it. And seeing Buster and Grandma together only reaffirmed my faith in the idea. After all, when I'd first laid eyes on Josh, I had felt some kind of energy rush through me, something deeper than simple attraction. And today's conversations only solidified it for me. I had no idea how Josh felt about me, but I wasn't as scared when thinking about talking to him.

That was something, right?

Almost home.

Approaching the alley, I instinctively tightened my grip on my pack.

I had conquered a fear today by talking to Josh, so I knew it would be out for blood.

A dog barked from inside the darkest depths, then turned to snarling as my steps brought me closer and closer to the blackened walls of brick. The darkness inside swirled like fog ready to suck all the light out of the world. I wondered how a place like this existed without the neighborhood wanting to tear it down. But I knew the answer to that question. Something like this couldn't *be* torn down, it had to be defeated. And my gut told me I was the only one who could, because somehow all my fears had created it in the first place.

My senses sharpened as I slowed down in fear. Halfway past, I searched inside the darkness, and footsteps headed toward me, loud and close, just like the night before.

Someone was in there.

Again.

And they were coming out.

A champion for the alley to finally materialize and take me down for good.

Maybe it was a good time to have that gun ready.

As I kept walking, I pulled the straps off my shoulders and began to unzip the backpack.

Almost past.

A man materialized out of the alley right next to his Wanted sign plastered to the side of the brick building. His expression matched that of the picture, cruel and hard, and his name had been torn off at the bottom.

This was the moment.

The alley was finally fighting back.

My biggest fear coming to life.

What happened to my parents was about to happen to me.

Every nightmare I'd imagined all wrapped up into one man.

And he was coming for me.

Moving fast now, I barely cleared the alley as I searched frantically inside my bag for the gun, but my hand kept hitting my sweater and sketchpad.

The sharp point of a blade pressed against my back, not enough to cut but enough for me to stop in my tracks.

"Give me your backpack," he demanded, his voice eerily gravelly.

You mean the backpack with an enormous revolver in it? My hand shook, still inside my bag.

"I said give me your backpack, bitch!" he yelled in my ear, and this time the tip of his blade punctured my skin.

"Okay, okay, don't hurt me," I cried.

Shakily, I began to hand him the backpack.

I can't give this man a gun! I can't give this evil a weapon!

The knife left my back as he reached for the pack.

I slammed my foot on his right toe with every ounce of force I had in me.

He grunted in surprise and pain, dropping the knife.

I pulled my backpack closer to my chest and kicked his knife, sending it flying into the street.

Where were the cars? Where were the people?

It was as if time had stopped and everyone had been plucked out of existence, leaving only me and this criminal, this warrior of the alley.

He recovered quickly from my attack and tackled me to the ground before I could run.

My hand was inside my backpack as I desperately searched with my fingers for the weapon that would save me from this monster.

The man yanked on my hand, trying to pry the backpack from me, and the way I kept the bag from him, he probably thought it held diamonds.

Panic threatened to overwhelm me, and it took all my power to stay conscious. After I kneed him in the groin, the man yanked his head back in pain, slamming it against the side of the brick wall. Anger renewed, he wrenched my hand out of my bag and pinned both hands down, blood trickling down his cheek and onto my shirt from the wound on his head.

Shaking his head in short bursts and blinking rapidly, he appeared to be trying to regain his focus. I took advantage of the moment and pulled one of my hands loose, reaching into my backpack again.

And there it was.

The gun.

My savior.

I couldn't think straight. I couldn't see straight. I wanted him off of me. I wanted to survive.

Jamming the revolver in his stomach, I pulled the trigger.

Blam!

The attacker fell limp on top of me.

I gasped for air and pushed him off with the last bit of strength I had.

The man lay on the ground, unmoving, blood streaming down his face.

I didn't know what to do.

Was he dead?

Was he dying?

Should I call for help?

Did I win?

Why weren't there people around to help me?

I needed help.

I . . . had to get home. I had to get away from him and the alley, his looming master behind us.

I threw the gun back in my bag and tried to slow my breathing. The short, quick, panicked breaths were making me dizzy. Scrambling to my feet, I stared down at his unmoving body.

I couldn't tell if he was breathing. I was too scared to check. I didn't think I'd make it through another attack. From where I stood though, his chest was still. Not even a twitch.

Not even a twitch.

He was dead.

He was dead.

He was dead.

One more time I searched for witnesses, but found none in sight. With one last glance at the attacker, I stared at the alley.

It was silent, not a single sound, the blackness impenetrable.

Was it trying to create another fighter? Another warrior to kill me?

I couldn't wait to see.

I ran.

Ran as fast as my legs would let me, the gun slapping against my side through my backpack.

I'd shot someone.

I'd killed someone.

I . . .

My mind jumbled into pieces.

I needed Grams.

Racing home, I swung the door open to our building, took the steps two at a time and finally let myself into our apartment. Bursting through the door, I was about to yell for Grandma when I saw her and Buster watching TV on the sofa, his arm wrapped sweetly around her shoulders.

The scene of such normalcy frazzled my brain. I wasn't sure how to react or feel.

Grandma turned to me and smiled, happier than I'd ever seen her, eyes twinkling with contentment. "Hi, sweetie. So? Did you have your conversation?"

Conversation?

I just killed a man.

I shot him.

I couldn't comprehend what she was asking me.

Grandma leaned her head to the side in concern, the expression on my face obviously alarming her. "Is everything okay?"

I couldn't ruin this for her. I couldn't take away her joy with my terror. Placing the backpack in front of me to cover my shirt and any signs I had been in a struggle, I forced a smile. "Fine. I'm totally fine." Then I acknowledged Buster with a small wave of my hand. "Hey, Buster."

Buster's eyes twinkled in the exact same way as Grandma's. They were in love, and they had just met. I could see it. I wouldn't let my horridness as a human being take any piece of bliss away from them.

Buster replied, "Howdy, Jeraline."

Blam!

The gun went off in my backpack, and a bullet hit Buster in the head.

I jumped.

Buster was fine, the gun safely tucked away.

I was losing it.

"Jeraline?" Grandma asked, her face crinkled with worry.

Trying my best to hide the turmoil within, I smiled with as much gumption as I could manage. "I'm going to bed. You guys have a good night."

Too afraid Grandma would see right through me and figure out what I had done, I didn't wait for a response. I hurried to my room and shut the door behind me.

Why did she give me this stupid gun?

But if she hadn't, would I still be alive right now? Did I save others by killing a man?

Bile reached the back of my throat.

No. I can't throw up. I won't throw up.

Swallowing it down, I sat on the edge of my bed and

opened my backpack, pulling out the revolver. My hands shook heavily, but I managed to put it back in the box and stuff it under my bed.

I barely had room to move in this space with the cutting table still out, so I crawled under the covers fully clothed. I didn't want to take off my clothes ever, as if it were armor protecting me. It was a strange thought, but a strong one, and I listened.

Police sirens grew louder and closer to my apartment.

They'd found me, and they were coming to arrest me.

Pulling the blankets over my head, I hid under the covers as if this would be enough to keep me hidden from the cops. The sirens faded in the distance, and I took a deep breath to try to regain some kind of composure.

There came the bile again. Swallowing it down once more, I poked my hand out from the blankets, still not ready to come up for air, and grabbed the picture of Josh off the end table, bringing it under the covers with me.

I didn't know why, but it gave me comfort.

I held on tight as I continued to breathe deep.

What was I going to do?

What was I going to do?

What was I going to do?

Breathe.

Stop shaking!

Breathe.

My life was over.

It was done.

The police sirens were back. I peeked out of my covers to

see flashes of red and blue light up my room in an eerie strobe effect. I ripped off my covers with my free hand, my other hand still holding the picture of Josh. Outside my window was an ocean of police cars.

A pounding on my door.

"Jeraline, the police are here to see you." Grandma's voice sounded worried and scared through the door.

I turned from the window, rooted in terror.

"Jeraline?" Grandma called my name again.

Without thinking, I quickly locked the door and hid under my blankets again.

The door handle rattled as Grandma tried to enter. "Jeraline, open this door right now. This is serious."

Grandma had no idea *how* serious. She was going to be so disappointed in me. How could she not? I was a murderer.

A loud thump from the door being kicked in followed by the footsteps of people piling into my bedroom. My blankets were yanked from my body, and I stared into the eyes of five glaring police officers, surrounding me in a circle.

"You have the right to remain silent . . ." He began his mantra, the rest of his words sounding distant and warbled.

I didn't struggle as they pulled me out of bed. The second officer took Josh's picture from my hands and handed it to another policeman. "What's this?" he asked.

To my shock, Rachel walked in and shook an accusing finger at me. "I knew it was you!"

The second police officer waved Josh's picture in front of me. "Add this to the list of charges."

The officer handed the picture to Rachel, who shook her

head in disappointment and satisfaction at finally catching me.

"No!" I screamed.

***

I awoke in a cold sweat.

It was a dream.

I searched my brain in hopes that shooting the man from the alley had been a dream as well. But no, it was real. He was dead because of me, and there was absolutely nothing I could do about it.

Picking up my cell phone, I checked the time: 3:32 a.m.

Trying to stop my body from shaking, I continued to breathe in deep, my eyes open.

What had I done?

10

OKAY, I ENTERED
(Happy now?)

My head hurt.

My body ached.

I think I'm paralyzed.

I moved my arm. Nope. I could move.

Everything that happened to me last night played over and over in my head. Maybe someone had seen what happened? Maybe the man hadn't died? Maybe . . .

I sat up in bed and grabbed my phone from the bedside table. Turning it on, I searched the internet for anything I could find on last night's events, but nothing came up. No dead body reports, no arrest reports, no gunshot reports, just a whole lot of nothing.

So what did that mean?

Did this really happen?

Had I made the whole thing up in my head?

I looked down at my shirt, still on from last night, and sure enough there was his blood. I remembered now. It had dripped from his head wound when he had me pinned down.

I choked, the memory too strong.

Ripping the shirt off of me, I grabbed a T-shirt from the floor and put it on.

My attacker was real.

It happened.

The alley may have sent him, but he existed. The flashback of his body pushing against mine, his hands trapping me to the ground . . . I shuddered, and my mouth burned from the acid crawling its way up my throat.

No. It was real.

So maybe if this guy was a wanted criminal, then the police might not report finding him dead? Maybe the cops would consider it a case of a bad guy getting killed by another bad guy. I could call the cops and ask, but I already knew I'd never do that.

Touching the bloodstain on my shirt caused my heart to race. Should I burn it? Should I just throw it away? Bleach! People always used bleach in the movies. I didn't have any bleach. I could get bleach. Did I really want to buy bleach? Could I please stop thinking about bleach!

Murderer.

I had to get this out of my head.

I'd go insane if I didn't.

If the police found me, then I'd accept the consequences. I wouldn't hide.

Yes.

Erasing what had happened wasn't an option, but shoving it deep down into the recesses of my brain and living in total denial seemed like a good idea right now.

I *needed* this to be the plan because the alternative?

Paralysis.

Terror.

Guilt so severe I wasn't sure how to live with myself.

Why had the alley done this to me?

Swallowing my feelings and emotions was something I was very good at.

Distractions.

I took the shirt and shoved it under my mattress. If the cops arrested me, I'd give them the shirt. Simple.

The design contest.

Before the attack, it had been my biggest source of fear besides Josh.

I hoped it was enough to distract me completely.

Reaching down to my backpack, I pulled out my sketchpad, thumbing through it until I found the flyer for the fashion contest. And now, staring at the flyer, entering and putting my work out there for all to see somehow didn't seem as scary after the terror of the attack last night.

Besides, going to Cassiopeia Design School was my dream, and this contest was the only reasonable path ahead of me.

And if I won, if I achieved my wish and was able to go to school, I was pretty sure it was the only way of defeating the alley for good.

It was a start anyway.

If I put my portfolio together quickly enough, I'd have time to stop by the Cassiopeia Design School to drop off my application before work.

It was a plan. I liked plans. They helped me forget.

Grabbing the empty portfolio notebook I had bought over a month ago from my desk, I carefully tore out each design from my sketchpad, cut off the perforated edges, and placed them inside the plastic sheaths until the portfolio was full. It was the best I could do considering I waited until the last moment. Stuffing the portfolio inside my backpack, I left my room, quickly made a couple of meals for me and Hank, placed them into my bag, and I was off. I didn't want to think about the fact that my Grandma wasn't up yet, because I didn't want to think about the fact that she may be in her bedroom with Buster. That thought almost erupted my brain like a volcano, so I shoved it aside as well and hurried out the door.

It was a ten-minute bus ride to the Cassiopeia Design School campus, and when I set foot on the grassy lawn of the school entrance, all thoughts of last night's attack melted away.

It had worked.

I had found the perfect distraction, the perfect bandage to cover and erase what had happened.

My insides vibrated with excitement. I belonged here. I felt it in my soul. It was home.

Resting in the center of the city, the school was a carved-out oasis of brick, ivy, and perfectly manicured lawns. Cobblestone walkways wended their way throughout the campus, giving the impression that the school was built long ago, but in reality, it was only a decade old. Large maple trees had been planted every twenty feet or so, giving much needed shade to anyone who wanted to spend their time outside on the black wrought-iron benches.

Surveying the intense beauty of it all only reiterated my disappointment that it was a school I could never afford.

Unless I won this contest.

A part of me was glad that the terror of the attack led me here. I wasn't sure I would have entered the contest otherwise. But thinking too much on that only caused the panic to rise up in me again, so I pushed it aside.

The flyer stated that applications were to be turned in at the admissions office, so I glanced at the posted campus map and headed in that direction. Passing by other students buzzing about, talking excitedly, I imagined them discussing their designs or a particularly great teacher or . . . anything. The potential of it all gave me a momentary glimpse of what my life could be like.

If I hadn't murdered someone.

Block. Blocking the thought and detaching.

Detach.

Breathe.

Good.

Grabbing the large silver door handle attached to one of the two ten-foot-high oak doors, I swung it open and walked down the hallway until I reached the admissions door and stopped.

This door was much plainer with respect to the rest of the campus. It was quite ordinary, blond wood, school logo, and shiny silver doorknob.

A turn of that knob and my path was set.

My hand began to shake uncontrollably.

Breathe.

Bringing up my trembling hand, I opened the door and entered the admissions office. There was a large leather couch and chair that faced the receptionist, who sat behind an enormous oak desk.

I could do this.

Nervously, I walked up to the receptionist, who was a beautiful woman with a planned messy bun and clothes that appeared to be casual but were perfectly placed to give the impression that she just naturally looked put together. My T-shirt and jeans weren't cutting it at the moment, especially for a fashion institute.

Acknowledging me as I approached her desk, the woman grinned in a way that said *I'm really busy. What do you want?* But what came out of her mouth was, "May I help you?"

I jumped back when her face morphed into my attacker from the alley.

As quickly as her face changed, it changed back, but now she glared at me with confusion. "Are you all right?" she asked.

Regaining my composure, I stuttered, "Um . . . sorry . . . is this where you enter the fashion contest?"

"Yes, hold on one minute." She opened a drawer and pulled out a form. "Fill that out. Do you have your portfolio?"

Nodding, I pulled my backpack from my shoulders.

"Perfect. Attach it to the form and turn it in here when you're done." The receptionist handed me a large clipboard.

Taking it, while now trying to balance holding my bag by the straps, was an ordeal, but once I had everything situated, I sat down on the leather couch.

Relieved to see that the application was only a page, I reached into my backpack and pulled out a pen to fill it out. My eyes briefly glanced at the window behind the receptionist.

My attacker stood outside, staring at me.

I closed my eyes, then opened them quickly.

He was gone.

Focus.

Fill out the form.

Luckily, a young woman walked into the office to distract me and approached the receptionist. "Hi. Could I get the application form for the fashion contest?"

"Of course," the receptionist said and handed her the form.

Plopping down next to me, the girl pulled out her portfolio to get it ready to turn in.

I gulped.

It was stunning.

As in, professional-level drawings that looked like they came from a top designer.

I finished the application and pulled out my own portfolio. They were child's drawings compared to the girl next to me.

I can't do this.

The exit door called to me, telling me to bolt.

As I was about to make a run for it, Emma from Jane Austen's book appeared at the door, standing in front of it.

"Don't even think about it. You're entering this contest." Emma eyed me sternly.

I shook my head, panicked.

"Yes, you are. Now get up and hand that application in with your drawings." Emma pointed to the receptionist with an air of command.

Taking another deep breath, I nodded, standing.

My legs ripped from the leather couch in a loud tearing sound.

Yup.

Flushed from embarrassment, I handed the receptionist my application that I attached to my portfolio. "Sorry," I said, though I had no grounds to be, but making a noise that sounded like a loud fart seemed like a good reason for an apology.

Before either woman responded, I hurried out of the office.

Once outside, it truly hit me.

I did it.

I entered the contest.

I was both elated and terrified. Now all I had to do was finish the dress for the pop-up fashion show on Thursday.

Which I hadn't even cut out the fabric for.

Which was a huge gown that would take hours of work.

Well, I said I needed a distraction. This would definitely fit the bill.

As I left the building, I noticed an art supply store next to the campus. I still had some time to spare before I'd be late for work, so I rushed over there and picked up some supplies for Hank. Not having a lot of money, I ended up buying an acrylic paint bundle, a couple different brushes (the cheaper ones; I had no idea paintbrushes cost so much!), and a small twelve-inch by twelve-inch canvas.

After purchasing the items, I stuffed them in my bag, raced to the bus station, and managed to catch the bus as it pulled up. Only a short time later I arrived at the bookstore, putting my bag in the locker, the meals in the fridge and arrived at the front counter with a wave to Josh.

Waving back, Josh opened his mouth as if he was about to say something when Rachel walked up, holding a framed picture in her hand. "Got your new Employee of the Month photo, Josh," Rachel beamed.

As Rachel placed the new picture on the wall, she glanced over her shoulder and threw me a knowing gaze.

Edmond appeared next to Rachel and the photo. "Your intuition is right. She definitely knows."

Rachel finished straightening the picture and turned toward me. "Much better, don't you think?"

Shyly, I smiled in agreement.

Edmond's gaze went from the new picture of Josh and back to Rachel. "You should steal this one too. Slowly make her go mad." He grinned.

Edmond disappeared as Rachel angled her head to the side in a satisfied way. Taking one last look at the picture, she smiled, then walked away.

The picture of Josh flashed into my attacker's Wanted poster. Turning abruptly away, I grabbed a piece of scratch paper and sketched the beginning of a design to occupy my thoughts elsewhere.

"Hey," Josh said.

I turned to Josh to see him smiling at me.

And there went my cheeks, burning with embarrassment, but I was relieved when his picture was no longer my attacker and was back to Josh's adorable face.

Josh didn't seem to notice as he glanced at the new picture of himself and groaned. "I was hoping she wouldn't replace that."

I knew she would, which was why I stole the first one. "She's really proud of you."

Shrugging, Josh answered, "I don't know why. I've literally

only been here three months, and I don't do anything more than you. Considering we're her only two employees, it's kind of weird."

It was totally weird, but very Rachel. After seeing the picture of Kent though, I did have an inkling as to why she treated Josh the way she did, so I shared. "I found a picture under the stacks of her and her kid, and he looks just like you. Maybe she doesn't talk to him anymore?"

"Great, so I'm some kind of surrogate?" Josh shifted uncomfortably.

"It's better than an unwanted stepchild."

Josh laughed, then turned thoughtful. "I don't think she leaves this building at all."

I glanced at the back of the store where Rachel had walked to and jumped with a start when my attacker stepped out of the stacks, staring straight at me.

"You okay?" Josh asked with concern.

The man was gone, never there to begin with. This plan to shove down what happened wasn't working out well for me.

"Fine. I thought I saw something." Ugh. Changing the subject back to Rachel, I said, "I wondered that about Rachel. I don't think I've seen her leave this building the entire time I've worked here."

After a moment of thought, Josh nodded. "Yeah, I haven't either. I tried to test the theory last night out of curiosity, to get her to come outside for a second, but she wouldn't budge, practically slammed the door in my face."

I paused, thinking. "That explains a lot." My heart squeezed with . . . sympathy? "Wanting to hide" was my middle name.

"What are you drawing?" Josh examined my sketch with interest.

Self-consciously, I covered the sketch with my hand.

"Sorry, none of my business." Josh lowered his head.

I was so mean.

"No. I'm sorry. I'm not used to showing anyone." I uncovered the page and shifted it in his direction for a better view. "It's one of my designs. I just entered a contest to try to get a scholarship to the Cassiopeia Design School. But I saw another girl's entry. I'm way out of my league."

Viewing the drawing more carefully, Josh said, "Don't be so hard on yourself. This is beautiful. Did you make this dress already?"

The sketch was another view of the dress I planned to make. "I started it, the pattern anyway. I have to wear it to the pop-up runway on Thursday. All the entries have to show one of their designs."

"Can I come?" he asked brightly.

What?

"If that's okay?" Josh took a step back, unsure.

Say something!

"Um, yeah, that sounds nice." I said that! I really said that.

Rachel walked up. "Jeraline, could you put the books in the cart back on the stacks?"

Weirdly, perfect timing. I wouldn't have to fumble my words after agreeing to let Josh come to the fashion show. "Yeah," I acknowledged.

I smiled at Josh as I pushed the cart away from the counter.

Well, that was a nice turn of events.

HE WALKED ME HOME!
(Can I puke now?)

Honestly, as weird as it sounded, placing books back in their proper spot was one of my absolute favorite tasks working at the bookstore. There was something so calming about escaping into the stacks surrounded by millions of characters and worlds that were more real to me than my own reality. And setting them where they were meant to be, where they were meant to be found by the perfect reader, made me feel like I was a part of something greater. It made me feel like I had a purpose.

It was magical.

As I pushed the cart around to the front to travel down another row of shelves, I caught Josh glancing at me from the counter, and in a moment of spontaneity and joy at what I was doing, I smiled at him.

The smile was returned, and a rush of giddiness flowed through me.

My head was full of dreamy thoughts until they screeched to a halt when I saw who was at the end of the aisle.

A police officer.

And he was coming my way.

I spun on my feet and dove behind a stray bookshelf that walled off a cozy reading nook. Poking my head out to see what the officer would do, luckily he hadn't noticed my leap.

What was I doing?

Had I really jumped behind a bookshelf to avoid an officer of the law? I couldn't help it though. Terror had replaced my blood at this point, because it was the only thing that pumped through my veins.

From the cover of my spying spot, I watched the cop pull out some kind of paper or picture from his wallet and show it to Rachel, who arrived at his side.

I didn't like the gleam in Rachel's eyes as she called out, "Jeraline?"

I shrunk back and squeezed my hands in panic. Dropping to the floor, I crawled down the opposite aisle until I found another good spot to hide. The mystery section, more specifically, three rows of Agatha Christie books. If Hercule Poirot couldn't save me, I didn't know who could.

But *should* I be saved?

I murdered a man, and this officer was simply doing his job. Why was I hiding? Why was I avoiding my punishment?

Speaking of the man, Hercule Poirot himself appeared next to me, standing over me like a pillar of judgment. He was older, from the '20s era, three-piece suit.

The only difference being that he stared down at me with

disappointment, shaking his head. "Really, Jeraline, this is very unbecoming of you. If this officer is a good detective, you will be caught and brought in for an accounting of your actions right away. Hiding in these . . . stacks . . . won't help you."

Guilt replaced fear, but then flipped right back to terror as I tried to ignore him and his stupid truthful words.

Rachel walked by without seeing me. "Where is that girl?"

That was too close.

Crawling down another row of stacks, Poirot followed me with more glares of disappointment. "This only makes you look guilty."

"I *am* guilty," I shot back.

I really, really was.

Poirot nodded, acknowledging my confession. "True, but there is a certain civilization in at least carrying yourself with some dignity. Turn yourself in. Now's your chance."

He was right. Now was the perfect opportunity to hand myself over to the authorities without anyone getting hurt. I almost stood up. I almost decided to do it.

But like the coward I was, I panicked and crawled down the aisle at full speed toward the front exit.

Poirot shook his head once more, then disappeared.

Arriving at the end of the aisle, I was about to make a mad dash for the door when a pair of legs stepped in my way.

Slowly, I cranked my neck up to see Rachel, glowering at me.

I managed a half laugh that sounded both creepy and absurd. "I . . ."

My fear and guilt turned to confusion as the officer finished paying for a book and left the bookstore.

I carefully stood up, embarrassed and befuddled.

Rachel stared at me as if I were an escapee from an insane asylum. "That nice officer needed your help, and you're here crawling on the floor? Did you hear me calling you?"

"No, I . . . didn't," I lied.

Eyeing me up and down, Rachel sighed, exasperated. "See that it doesn't happen again."

"Yes, ma'am."

Rachel left toward the back of the store, and I ran a hand through my hair trying to calm my frazzled nerves.

As the officer walked by the window, he turned toward me, staring into my soul, recognition in his eyes.

He pounded on the window in slow motion, his voice distorted. "Murderer!"

I jumped back, and the officer was as he was before, normal speed, walking past the window and out of view.

Rooted to the ground, I tried to move, to function, to do *anything.*

Edmond materialized in front of me, placing his hands on my shoulders. "You defended yourself. You are not a murderer."

My mouth was dry, and my throat felt as if it were closing. Edmond's words weren't registering.

"Jeraline?" Edmond shook my shoulders not so gently. "Snap out of it. You have a life to live."

I found my voice. "How can I? When I ended someone else's?"

"By taking one step at a time, physically and mentally. You may have ended that criminal's life, but it wasn't intentional. It was survival. As you survived that moment, you *will* survive this moment." Edmond kept his eyes trained on mine.

I pushed down my overwhelming feelings of dread and guilt and forced myself to walk toward the counter. Edmond disappeared with an expression of concern on his face.

Not even seeing Josh could force the ache in my stomach to go away as I approached him. Before I made a fool of myself, I nodded toward the stacks and my abandoned cart. "I better finish."

Innocent and kind eyes sparkled in greeting, and Josh offered, "You need any help?"

"No, I'm good. Thanks, though."

I left for the stacks.

Shockingly, the rest of the day proceeded without mishap. I began to feel almost normal again as we locked up for the night.

Entering the night air, with garbage in one hand, my backpack full of art supplies and dinner for Hank in the other, my fears had subsided a bit for calmness. I decided to enjoy the moment.

Tossing the garbage in the dumpster, I searched for Hank. "Hank?"

Stepping up next to the dumpster wasn't Hank, it was my attacker.

Backing up in fear, all the terror rushed back to me.

"Jeraline?" My attacker morphed into Hank, his expression concerned. "I didn't mean to scare you."

Mortified at what Hank must have thought, I shook my head, stepping forward. "No, Hank, I'm sorry. I'm a bit jumpy lately. Here."

Pulling out the plastic bag full of art supplies and Hank's dinner from my backpack, I handed them to him.

Hank stared at the art supplies in the bag, his voice quiet as he said, "I didn't think you'd do it."

"What do you mean? You promised me a painting." I pretended not to understand his doubts, but my body tightened at the thought that he'd questioned my sincerity.

Breathing deep, Hank beamed. "I will start tonight."

That was when I noticed how clean Hank was and that his clothes appeared fresh and new. "Hey, you got new clothes." I didn't want to make a big deal of it, not sure how insecure he might be.

But he had an air of assurance that I'd only ever seen when he talked of the past. "I found a nice shelter a few blocks from here near the hospital. They gave me clothes and a shower. I can't go every day, but at least I have a nice bed to look forward to a couple times a week."

Warmth spread through my limbs at the thought of Hank having a place to rest his head. Even if it wasn't every night like he deserved, at least it was something. "That's great, Hank." And it meant he was safer, because he wouldn't be in the shadows where men like my attacker lay in wait. I shook the thought from my head. "Extra cookies again." I pointed toward the paper bag of food.

Hank seemed calmer, happier. He tipped his imaginary hat as he liked to do. "Thank you, Jeraline."

"Of course. Friday's my next shift. See you then?"

Hank nodded, happy. "See you Friday. I might have your painting ready for you by then."

That perked me up. "Don't rush, but that makes me so excited! I can't wait to see it!"

Waving as he left, Hank walked a little prouder than normal.

Standing by the dumpster, holding my backpack, I didn't need to go back inside. I could leave. It was for the best since I had left things as good as to be expected with Josh, and with all my insanity I didn't want him to think less of me.

Because killing someone could definitely change one's opinion.

Yeah.

Walking toward home, I had almost passed the bookstore when . . .

"Jeraline?" Josh's voice called out to me.

Was this a fantasy? Was I making this up in my head? I couldn't tell anymore.

Turning around, I saw Josh hurry to catch up to me. No declaration of love, no tuxedo or dance floor. It was real, which meant messing it up was still an option.

"Let me walk you home," he offered with a grin.

Panic.

Observing my obviously conflicted expression, he added, "I'd feel better if you'd let me."

Where was he last night?

But I decided to go with it. "Okay."

Josh reared his head back slightly, as if he had been ready for a counterargument. "Oh . . . great. I had expected more of a fight."

"Am I that horrible?" I asked in disgust at myself.

"Not horrible at all. Stubborn, you're more stubborn I'd say." He laughed.

We began our walk toward my apartment, and lo and behold . . .

No talking.

So uncomfortable.

I needed to do something. Small talk. Anything.

The silence was reaching sweaty palm levels.

Intervention needed to happen.

I should fall, trip, be clumsy, anything to break the tension.

But Josh decided to be blunt. "Do you *not* like me?"

Knots tied themselves over and over in my stomach. "No!" That was it. That was all I had to say about that apparently.

"No you don't, or no you do?" Josh clarified like a normal human.

Which I wasn't.

"I do like you." Smooth.

"Because one minute we're having awesome conversations, and the next you look at me like I'm a leper." Josh said this lightheartedly, but I could tell it was laced with insecurity.

Because I was a horrible person.

"I . . . I didn't mean . . . I just have trouble . . . talking . . . and there are other things . . ." Nobel laureate here.

Awkward silence.

Shocker.

The presence of the alley made itself known with a growling in the darkness as we arrived in front of it.

Shivering, Josh noticed the alley with trepidation. "You walk by here every night?"

The shadow of my attacker materialized in the blackness of the alley, and I jumped back, but he quickly disappeared. There was no way the alley would take this walk with Josh away from me. I wouldn't let it.

"Are you okay? That's the second time today you've jumped for no reason." Josh looked at me with concern.

Trying to hide my terror and nerves, I explained in a lie. "Just nervous for . . ." Think of something. Think of something. ". . . the runway show." Yes. Good one. "And I'm a bit odd around people I don't know. I never quite fit in right." I went for honesty.

And to my surprise, Josh answered, "Me too."

"But you're perfect," I responded, appalled.

Oh God.

Kill me now.

"I mean, I don't see that."

"I'm far from perfect. I dropped out of college, live with my brother, and work retail all while trying to write a book that I'm pretty sure I'll never finish because apparently I have zero self-discipline. Living the dream." Josh sighed in frustration.

It made me laugh, which in turn made Josh laugh.

"I work retail too, you know."

"But you seem to love it. Not the work, but being in the store, surrounded by books. I wish I had that same kind of passion, and I'm supposed to be the writer. I used to love books more than anything, and now I look at them and they just make me . . . jealous." Josh's expression was heartbroken, and all I wanted to do was make him feel better.

"Maybe the books remind you that you haven't finished yours? Maybe if you let that guilt go, you could find your love of writing again?" What was I, a therapist? What on earth made me say that?

But Josh didn't get defensive or lash out, he stared ahead, contemplative. "That actually makes a lot of sense." Passing the alley, Josh asked, "Do you live by yourself?"

"No, I live with my grandma. I have since I was nineteen."

"That's sweet. What about your parents? Do they live nearby?" Josh asked innocently.

"My parents died, another reason I live with Grams." Why did I tell him that? I was getting way too personal. Someone please stick a piece of duct tape on my mouth.

"I'm sorry . . . I'm really sorry."

"It's okay. It's not your fault. They were killed in a mass shooting at a grocery store." Stop talking!

Halting in his tracks, Josh's entire body language changed. He lifted his hand, reaching for mine.

Was he was going to try to comfort me?

A gunshot rang in my ear.

Josh's face morphed into my attacker.

Luckily, I snapped out of it and pretended not to see his offered hand. "My grandma is great. I'm lucky to have her."

Josh took his hand back, his eyes downcast, then responded, "Yeah."

"Well, this is it."

We stood in front of my apartment building.

Josh reached down to the ground and picked up a penny, handing it to me. "For luck." He gently squeezed my hand shut over the penny.

Knees. Numb. Going to pass out.

I turned my head and stepped toward the door of my building. "Thanks for walking me home."

"Anytime." Josh smiled.

Another awkward moment, shuffling. What was wrong with

me? I had to get inside before I ruined everything.

Waving nonchalantly, I opened the door to the building. "Good night."

Josh waved back. "See you at the fashion show."

As I entered the building, I poked my head out one last time and said, "I do, Josh. I do like you."

Then I shut the door in his face.

Classic.

12

UM. EXCUSE ME? WHAT?
(Grandma! Impulsive much?)

alking up the stairs to our apartment, my
brain was goo.

I do, Josh. I do like you. Really? And
then what? Run inside my building like
an absolute crazy person. I hoped I didn't freak him out. But to
be fair, walking me home was quite an ambush. I hadn't been
prepared at all for things like conversations or acting normal in
any way. It was completely unfair.

Slowing down, I reached the front door and opened it.

Grandma walked out of her bedroom decked out in dancing
gear. "I've been waiting for you." She walked over to the record
player and put on a waltz.

My grandma was the sweetest.

I really needed this. "Hold on, just a second."

I placed my backpack by my bedroom door, then strode over
to Grandma's open arms, and we began to dance. She had taught

me so many different kinds of dances over the years: waltz, tango, rumba, samba, mambo, quickstep, a little swing. Buster was one lucky guy if he owned any dancing shoes, and if he didn't, I was sure Grandma would start his lessons soon. It had been her favorite thing to do when Grandpa was alive. They had even won a few amateur competitions in their day.

When Grandma first brought up the idea of teaching me to dance, it had been a month after my parents' death. I had honestly not wanted to do a single thing, let alone learn how to dance. But she had forced me to my feet and taught me a simple two-step waltz.

It had been so freeing. It made me forget, if only for a moment, what had happened. My grandmother always knew exactly how to help me, to make me feel better. And now when I danced, I allowed myself complete immersion, which lately meant imagining myself dancing with Josh in some fairy-tale landscape or another.

But in this moment, I just wanted to be with Grams.

"Did you have a good day?" she asked.

I went with honesty. "I haven't decided yet."

Watching my grandmother's face light up filled me with delight as she said, "You did it, didn't you? You talked to Josh!"

Laughing as she twirled me in a spin, I answered, "I did. I actually talked to him yesterday too, but you and Buster looked so cozy I didn't want to interrupt." *And I didn't want to tell you I shot someone.* Swatting the thought away so as to not ruin the moment, I continued, "He walked me home tonight."

Grandma pulled me in with an ear-to-ear grin. "That's wonderful! Did he kiss you good night?"

"Oh God no. We barely talked." The horror and beauty of that actually happening overwhelmed me. I sighed, exasperated. "I don't know what to do. I'm twenty-two years old, and I'm acting like I'm fifteen."

Giving me another twirl, Grams said kindly, "Shy is shy. It doesn't matter what age you are, trust me on this. But if you can muster up the courage, tell him you like him."

It only happened ten minutes ago, and I was already having flashbacks. "I did. And he didn't say anything."

Grandma laughed. "Knowing you, you didn't give him a chance to. You tucked tail and ran before he uttered a response. Am I right?"

Hey, no fair knowing me that well.

I had done exactly that. If our outside door had the capability of slamming shut, it would have as I booked it up the stairs.

I was such a coward.

Pulling me back in from a spin, Grandma smiled. "I knew it. Next time, give him a chance to say something. You're so beautiful inside and out. I wish you could see that."

"I just . . . don't see myself that way."

Sighing, Grandma nodded. "No one does for some messed up reason, but that's why I'm here. To push you. And to remind you that whether you believe it or not, you're gorgeous."

Grandma stopped the dance to hold my shoulders and look me in the eye. "You and I are so much alike. Don't be so scared of life that you miss it."

Behind her, my attacker floated behind the window, blood oozing down his face.

Grandma's forehead creased in concern. "What's wrong?"

Instead of answering her directly, I asked, "What would you do if you shot someone?"

"Oh. I wasn't expecting that turn in our conversation." Grandma sat down on the couch, and I sat next to her.

"I know, but I've been thinking about it lately." Think of an excuse. Think of an excuse. "Because of the gun you gave me."

Grandma nodded, and her expression turned thoughtful. "I guess it would depend on who it was."

"A criminal, someone attacking you."

"Honestly? I'd like to hope that I'd take the moral high ground, but I don't know if I would. People like that took away my daughter and your father. I hate that I think this way, but I feel like anyone who would murder someone of their own free will deserves to die." Grandma leaned back on the couch as if this revelation shocked her.

"You wouldn't feel guilty?" Because right now, I felt like dying.

"If it's me or him? And he attacked me? I'd rather it be him. There are a lot more people who'd want me around than a killer. It's why I got you that gun. You may need to defend yourself someday. We should sign you up for lessons," Grandma insisted.

Lessons. For a gun I'd already fired into a human being.

Why hadn't I waited? And what if I had? Would I even be here to contemplate that answer? Or would I be dead in front of the alley from Hell?

"Jeraline?" Grandma leaned her head sideways, sudden worry on her face.

When my eyes met hers, her brows furrowed in confusion. "Some police officers stopped by looking for you."

111

Fists pounded on the front door, and I jumped off the couch.

"Open up! Police!" A muffled shout from outside.

"It looks like they're here again." Grandma shrugged as if it was a typical weeknight.

This was it.

I had to confess.

I had to tell her my side of the story before she'd never speak to me again. "Grandma, I shot a man with the gun. He attacked me. I protected myself, like you said."

With a loud bang, the police busted down the door. Five officers raced in, guns leveled straight at me. Two of them holstered their guns and grabbed my arms, handcuffing my hands behind me. My knees gave in and I collapsed, but they held me up as they dragged me toward the door.

And Grandma watched, shaking her head in disappointment.

"Grandma," I barely choked out, tears falling down my cheeks.

With a bright flash of light, I was back on the couch with Grandma as she stared at me with a different kind of disappointment. It was the kind where her expression screamed that *she* had disappointed *me*.

"I had no idea you'd take it this hard." Grandma's voice was barely above a whisper.

I shook my head to rid myself of the imagined nightmare and tried to focus on what she was saying to me. "Take what hard . . . ? I'm sorry, what?"

"Jeraline, are you sure you're okay? You look like you're going to pass out, and you're sitting down."

"I am feeling a bit dizzy." Everything was falling apart, but

I needed to know why Grandma kept staring at me as if I had kidnapped her puppy. Taking a few deep breaths, more for show than for actual help, I focused on her and her only. "Now what did you say?"

Grandma reached over and held my hands in hers. "I said I'm moving in with Buster."

A bomb might as well have exploded in my face. "What!"

"Buster. We're going to move in together at his house. I'm moving my stuff over there tomorrow."

I no longer felt faint.

I was livid.

"Tomorrow? That's insane! You've been on one date! You just met him!"

Tightening her grip on my hands, Grandma continued as if I hadn't yelled at her for losing her mind. "I don't have very many things. I'm leaving all the furniture and everything else here for you."

She wasn't listening.

She couldn't hear me.

She didn't *want* to hear me.

But I had to make her see that what she was doing was dangerous. It was worse than that. It was . . . I didn't know what, but it was bad. "You're completely rushing into this. Do you even really know Buster all that well?"

At least she addressed this, but not to my liking. "Roberta and Claire have known Buster for twenty years. He's a good man, Jeraline. And besides, you know your parents got engaged the first day they met and moved in together two weeks later."

I was a cornered animal, feral and needing to lash out. "At

113

least they waited two weeks!" Yeah, I knew that was a failed argument, so I yelled, "This is absurd! It's crazy! It's reckless!"

Grandma laughed, momentarily breaking my tirade, her laughter had that effect on me, though a part of me wanted to hold on to all my terror and rage. Pulling my hands up to her face, she kissed them with affection. "You're probably right, but I'm trying to take my own advice and live life to the fullest. I can't be scared anymore. And I know it's quick, but when you know, you know."

Brain freeze.

Body freeze.

Grandma pulled me into a hug.

I cracked.

My mind cracked.

And all I could do was stay in Grandma's arms, holding her tightly—maybe then she'd stay.

"I love you more than life itself, you know that, right?" she whispered in my ear.

Tears fell freely down my face as I nodded into Grandma's shoulder. "I love you, too, Grandma."

I needed to let go.

I needed to let her have this.

I couldn't be the reason she stopped living her life.

Pulling back, I stood, separating from her completely. I managed a smile. "I really am happy for you, Grandma. I just need to process this."

She answered, "Of course. I understand completely." Grandma couldn't hide the sadness from her face at my reaction. I couldn't let her feel that way. I needed to make it right even if I didn't feel it was right.

I just didn't know how.

So, I did what I always did in tough situations. I changed the subject.

Leaning down, I kissed the top of her head. "I'm going to work on my dress. The runway show is on Thursday."

Grandma didn't skip a beat. She reached up and squeezed my hand. "Okay, sweetie. I have a good feeling about it." Then she made sure our eyes met. "And Jeraline? It's time for you to be happy too."

Happy?

It seemed like such a dream, I wasn't sure it was possible.

I was losing the only support I had in the world right when it was falling apart.

But I refused to let her see that, so I nodded, kissed her cheek and walked to my room.

Maybe sewing would help fill this growing hole in the pit of my stomach.

TEA LEAVES
(And not the yummy kind, the tell-your-future kind, which is way more creepy!)

I should turn myself in.

I should turn myself in.

I should turn myself in.

Grandma didn't need me anymore. She was leaving me. Maybe jail would be better?

As I gently closed my bedroom door the rest of the way, I came face-to-face with my fold-out table. It still had paper strewn on its surface with a few pattern pieces already cut out. I was way behind. I had tonight and tomorrow to make a dress good enough to win a scholarship to the school of my dreams.

I wanted it to be beautiful.

Which was kind of hard right now because I was sinking into a mud pit of despair.

Focus.

It was obvious I wasn't about to turn myself in. Whether that was from terror or denial I hadn't sorted through yet.

So yeah.

Dress.

Focus.

Focus.

I couldn't focus.

I was about to lose everything.

Focus.

Grabbing the tape measure, I went on autopilot, drawing lines, roughing out the bodice pieces, then cutting them out. I wanted the bottom half of the dress to be huge, and my room wasn't big enough to create an actual pattern, so I cut out multiple long, full circle pieces that draped to the floor with a smaller circle on top. That way when I sewed the small circles together, they would create the exact size of my waist. Then all I'd have to do would be to attach the giant skirt to the bottom of the bodice.

Sounded easy.

But took forever.

Creating the pattern became almost hypnotic, as I knew my own measurements so well and had patterned so many dresses over the years. Before I knew it, I was clearing the table off and laying the fabric down, cutting out the pieces for the dress. Grabbing some interfacing, I cut that out too, the stiff under-fabric that would make the bodice perfectly shaped. With a quick glance at my notions shelf, I was relieved that I had enough boning to sew onto the bodice as well. Boning was made of thick woven nylon that, when sewn into the vertical seams of a corseted bodice, would give it the rigidity it needed.

Glancing at my phone, the clock said it was midnight.

I could go a couple more hours.

Everything all cut out, now for assembly.

It took almost the full two hours to sew all the basic pieces together, the sound of the machine almost hypnotic and relaxing as it punctured into the fabric.

A rush of relief pulsed through me as I had at least the semblance of a dress in front of me. The bodice had taken the longest, since sewing in boning and a lining always took time even when I was going fast, but the bottom half was simply a lot of long seams. I didn't have time to make a petticoat for such a large gown, so I'd have to buy one. There was a store not far from my house that sold them.

Two a.m.

I should go to bed, but I was wide awake. Sudden inspiration hit me, and I fumbled through my notions shelf once more until I found what I was looking for: tiny, eighth of an inch in diameter crystal beads. Sparkling like diamonds, I began to sew them on the bottom half of the dress where the bigger stars were printed on the fabric. Was I adding extra work on myself? Yes. Would it be worth it to see the universe sparkle all around me as I walked down the runway? Absolutely.

Beading was difficult and time consuming, and I'd never have time to fully bead the entire skirt, but I'd at least place the crystals on the largest constellations.

As I sewed a diamond on the star my parents named after me, I glanced over at their picture by my bedside. Instead of them dancing on top of the Empire State Building, they were lying dead on the ground, blood pooling around their bodies.

Snapping out of my delusion, I continued to bead the dress, my eyes welling up with tears that fell onto the fabric.

118

Before I completely soaked the dress, I needed to stop.

Placing the unfinished dress on my cutting table, I sat on the edge of my bed and picked up the picture of Josh.

It was time.

I needed to return this.

Stealing a picture and displaying it at my bedside was at best weird and at worst stalkerish.

"I'll return you. No more fantasies." Stuffing it quickly into my backpack, I zipped it up before I could change my mind.

And though my eyes were wide open, I lay in bed hoping sleep would find me.

***

Grandma put the last of her things into Buster's car, which basically equated to clothes and some knickknacks. She wasn't kidding when she said she'd leave everything for me. I did my best to not appear sulky, but I was almost positive I failed miserably.

Grams was leaving.

Really leaving.

Buster came around from behind with another pile of clothes. "This is the last of it."

"Put it on top of those boxes," Grandma instructed, and he quickly did as he was told.

Turning to me, Grandma gave me a once-over, then hugged me tightly. "Don't be scared. This will be an adventure."

"I should be saying that to you." And I should. But all my wires were crossed lately.

Walking to the passenger side of the car, Grandma said,

"Well, I'm saying it to you."

I rushed to her side once more and hugged her again.

She whispered in my ear, "You're going to be okay."

Pulling away, Grams gave me one last squeeze of encouragement and sat inside the car. "More than okay. You're going to win that contest tomorrow, and your dreams of fashion school will finally happen. I just know it."

Why did that make me more nervous than excited?

"Speaking of which . . ." I shut the car door. Her window was rolled down though, and I continued. "I should get to finishing the dress," I said, hoping the terror wasn't obvious in my eyes.

"Well, so far, it's the most stunning piece you've ever created. You're a shoo-in." Grandma winked as she buckled her seatbelt.

As Buster slid into the driver's seat, he waved to me. "We'll see you tonight for dinner."

Nodding, I waved good-bye.

And they were off, driving down the road and away from *me*.

With a loud sigh, I entered the building and went up the stairs. The runway show was tomorrow, and I needed to finish this dress.

Plopping down on my chair, I pulled layers and layers of fabric toward me until I reached the bottom of the skirt. Time to hem. Placing it under the sewing machine, I clamped down the presser foot and began to sew the endless hem. The further I'd sew, the more fabric appeared. Hours passed as the never-ending hem kept going and going, until finally the bottom of the dress was finished. Breathing a sigh of relief and satisfaction, I moved on to the detail work of the bodice and skirt.

One bead at a time, each one hand-sewn onto the surface, I

felt as if I were a god creating my own universe. I'd been at it so long that when I glanced at the time, I gasped in panic. If I didn't leave now for Buster's, I'd be horribly late. And as cautious as I was about Grandma moving in with a complete stranger, I still wanted to make a good impression.

Typing the address into my phone, I was relieved that it was in walking distance, only a few miles. I could take the bus, but the early evening air would do me good, clear my head.

Grabbing my keys, I left the apartment building and followed the map on my phone.

The sun lowered on the horizon, still an hour or so from setting, but by the time I reached Buster's, the sky was streaked with deep oranges and reds. It was calming, peaceful, and for a few seconds I was able to clear my mind of the stress of what I had done and of what was to come.

Buster's house had charm much like its owner, with bright red trim around the door and windows and a deep gray, painted on the wood-slatted walls of the one-story house. Three steps led up to a front porch that spanned the length of the house, with a swinging bench on one side and a couple of wicker chairs and a broken tile-mosaic-topped table on the other. I knew already that Grandma and Buster would spend a lot of summer nights out here on this porch. The neighborhood was suburban, with other houses of unique designs and color schemes, not the cookie cutter houses that seemed to be the norm nowadays.

As the sun sank behind the hills, the light grew dimmer and I had a full view of Buster's front window.

I stopped at the sight in front of me. In the living room, Buster and Grandma waltzed across the floor in perfect unity.

Affection radiated through my body at seeing them so happy, and yet an oppressive weight pushed down on my chest at the same time.

I had been replaced.

Sighing, I walked up to the front door and knocked.

Moments later, Buster opened the door and smiled at me warmly. "Howdy do, Jeraline. Come on in."

Entering Buster's house, it was as charming as the outside—a living room on the right, a bedroom door in the back center, and the dining room on the left with a swinging door that led to what I would assume was the kitchen. The furniture was old and sturdy, like Buster. Some of Grandma's boxes littered the floor next to the bedroom door, but nothing that would take long to unpack.

Holding his hand out, Buster pointed to the round dining table with steaming hot food resting on its surface. "Right on time. Let's all sit."

My tummy grumbled at the display: pot roast and gravy served with potatoes au gratin and sautéed carrots. I hadn't realized how hungry I was. Sitting down, I managed to say, "This looks amazing, thank you."

Buster and Grams shared a smile, and Buster replied, "You're very welcome. Now dig in."

***

Afterward, I was sure my stomach would burst open from fullness. Buster walked through the swinging door (which I was right, it did lead to the kitchen) and came out holding a tray with three large cups of tea. I had asked for Earl Grey and was thrilled when I saw the metal strainer indicating it was loose leaf. As he placed the cup in front of me, the rich and fragrant smell filled me with warmth. "This smells delicious. Thank you, Buster."

"My pleasure," he responded and sat down after handing a mug to Grandma and taking one himself.

Dinner conversation had been small talk about the move and the weather, but now Grandma gave me a look that suggested things were about to get serious. "Jeraline? Buster and I were wondering if you could help him reshingle the roof. I know you used to help with your father's handyman work when you were younger, and it's going to start raining soon."

What?

Wasn't expecting that.

"I barely remember how." I tried to hide the befuddlement from my tone.

Buster smiled at me as if to say *Trust me, this wasn't my idea*, then eased my mind when he said, "I worked at a roofing company for twenty years or so. I just need an extra set of hands?"

The image of Buster trying to shingle this house by himself made my palms sweat. "Yes, of course. You'll have to remind me of what to do."

With a genuine nod of gratitude, Buster answered, "I appreciate it."

Taking out the loose leaf strainer, I placed it on the tray.

"Well, now." Buster perked up and took the strainer full of Earl Grey. "I used to be able to read these things. An old gypsy taught me how. What do you say, Jeraline? Want to know your future?"

No.

"Sure, why not?"

"Now, this is exciting," Grandma chimed in.

Buster put on his reading glasses and dumped the tea leaves onto the table in front of him. He studied them for a good few minutes. Sweat dripped down my neck. Why was this so stressful?

A strange look crossed his face.

Oh man. Every muscle tensed in anticipation.

I couldn't hold back. "What do they say?"

"Yes, Buster, what's Jeraline's future?" Grandma gave me a wink of encouragement.

But Buster used a napkin to gather the wet tea leaves and placed them back on the tray with a forced smile. "I guess I forgot how. Getting old."

Nuh-uh.

He had seen something.

Grabbing the now soaked napkin full of Earl Grey, I searched for answers, but all I saw was a glump of brown.

"Okay, now you're both making a mess." Grandma shook her head in mock annoyance. Picking up the napkin of tea, she placed it back on the tray and stood. "I'm going to put this in the kitchen." And with that, Grams left the two of us alone for a moment.

"I know tea leaves and tarot may seem silly to you, but sometimes they show things. Usually they're just pulling on the person's energy, their thoughts, if that makes sense." Buster's expression was one of concern, which of course then made me concerned. Why was he telling me this?

"So you *did* see something?" I prodded cautiously.

"I saw what the leaves picked up from you," he said cryptically, then sighed. "You know, Jeraline, I served in Vietnam," Buster said out of the blue. Where was this coming from?

"I didn't know," I answered lamely.

"It was the scariest time of my life. Not because people were trying to kill me; that I could handle. It was because I was shooting back."

Hercule Poirot appeared next to Buster. "The chap has figured you out."

My eyes went toward the swinging kitchen door, as I wanted to grab the pile of tea to try to read it again.

Buster cleared his throat, regaining my attention. "You're sent to war to murder, and you come back to live a normal life, like it didn't happen, like you didn't kill fifteen souls. I remember each and every one of them. Their faces are burned into my memory forever."

Hercule gave me a solemn shake of the head. "You really should turn yourself in."

I sat so still, my breath held, forgetting how to function.

He continued, "There's nothing more terrifying than taking another human being's life, even if it is to save yours."

Shaking his head in disappointment, Hercule said, "There is no justification for murder." With that, Hercule Poirot disappeared back into the ether.

What do I do?

What do I tell him?

Grandma? How long does it take to put a tray down and come back?

"I can't imagine," I answered, knowing full well I didn't have to. I had lived it.

Buster's expression was kind and sympathetic, which only frightened me more. "I'm sure you could."

Grandma's voice cut the quiet. "It's such a beautiful night. We should go out on the porch."

I jumped back in my seat on reflex. Not wanting Grandma to think anything was wrong, I began to gather the plates on the table. "I've got this. You guys enjoy the night."

Buster took Grandma's hand, then turned to me. "If you ever need someone to talk to, I'm here for you. I know we just met, but I'm a good listener."

I didn't answer.

I couldn't.

What could I say?

Watching the two of them head outside, I was filled with dread.

Buster knew, or strongly suspected at the least, yet he had said nothing.

Maybe that meant I could trust him.

I didn't know for sure.

Bringing the dishes into the kitchen, I knew it would only be a matter of time before my secret was out anyway.

I prayed I wouldn't fall apart before then.

THE FASHION SHOW
(Otherwise known as total humiliation.)

I entered the apartment and flipped on the lights. My hands were full with a large bag that contained the biggest petticoat I'd ever seen. It was all smooshed up at the moment, but this gown was going to be enormous. Placing the bag down at my feet, I got a good look at the apartment.

The TV was off, and Grandma was gone.

Locking the door behind me, I needed to leave the living room. It reminded me too much that I was alone.

Walking into my bedroom, I maneuvered past my cutting table and sat on the edge of my bed, peering out the window. A few of the lights were on in the building next door, and a flash of movement caught my eye. A couple danced and then kissed in a perfect romantic moment.

Emma appeared next to the window, staring at the couple.

"Jealous?" I asked her.

The man dipped the woman, and they both laughed, in love.

"Definitely," Emma sighed.

As I watched the couple with the same yearning as Emma, the man's face distorted into my attacker.

Nearly falling off the bed from the sight, I glanced back up at the couple, but my attacker was gone, just another stranger dancing with his partner. I pulled down the shutters.

Emma focused on me. "Runway show is tomorrow."

Standing up, I grabbed the dress and plopped down on the chair next to my sewing machine. Taking a threaded needle, I began sewing on more crystals. "I'm almost done. Only a few more of these diamonds."

After another hour of hand sewing, the beading was done, and I hung the dress on the door.

"It's beautiful," Emma admired.

"I can't believe I finished it." I really couldn't. But it was as magical as I'd imagined it would be.

"Better get some sleep. You need your beauty rest. You are going to be modeling tomorrow," Emma positively beamed.

I groaned, "Don't remind me."

Putting the dress into a garment bag, the zipper barely made it up, it had so much fabric. Crawling into bed, I tried to shut out all the noise in my head as I closed my eyes.

Please don't screw this up.

***

Feeling it was serendipity, I walked up to the renovated warehouse that normally housed bingo but would now be the location of the runway show. The gigantic neon sign on the roof was a weird sense of comfort as I entered the large opening. All the picnic tables had been stacked against the wall and in their place was a judging booth on the left (right on top of the bingo stage) and a long makeshift runway down the center surrounded on both sides with fold-up chairs filled with people. Curtains framed the front of the runway, and according to the email I had received two days ago but read for the first time this morning, that was where I was supposed to go.

Carrying the garment bag in my arms was difficult. Together the dress and petticoat weighed about thirty pounds. This was going to be a spectacle. I just hoped it was a spectacle the judges would like. At least I had already done my hair and makeup before I left, hence why I was running late.

I glanced at the clock on the wall. The show was about to start soon.

Hurrying through the curtains and trying not to knock them down with the bulk of my dress was a challenge, but I finally pushed my way inside.

Packed with models and designers getting ready, the sight sent my heart straight to my toes.

What was I doing here?

As I was about to run screaming, Grandma arrived and walked over to me, giving me a much-needed hug.

All my nervousness spilled out in one sentence, "I'm so late and the show is about to start and I'm not dressed yet."

Grandma forced me to look at her by holding onto my arms. "Deep breaths. You're going to be fine. Your hair and makeup are already done, and it'll take you two minutes to get into your gown." Then she winked at me with a conspiratorial glint in her eyes. "And I've been here a while and have seen the other contestants, you've got this in the bag."

"Grandma, you don't know that." I appreciated her support, but observing all the models in front of me made my mind squeeze with embarrassment. "Oh man, I should've hired a model."

Tightening her grip on my arms, Grandma said, "I saw your dress before it was even finished, and it blows all these other designers out of the water. You're going to be the star, and you *are* a model. It's better showing off your own design anyway." Glancing over her shoulder toward the closed curtain, she turned back to me with an eyebrow raised in excitement. "That boy, Josh, from the picture you stole is here. I gather you two have been talking some more?"

Gulp.

"He actually came?" I peeled away from Grandma's embrace and approached the curtain, still lugging my dress. I peered outside.

I must have walked straight past him. He sat by himself in the second row of chairs, shifting in his seat and wringing his hands.

On the loudspeaker, a voice boomed, "All contestants have your models or yourselves report to the start of the runway."

The curtain dropped, and my eyes widened in terror.

Grandma grabbed the garment bag out of my arms and helped me get dressed in comic speed. Though there were vanities and mirrors all around, I was too scared to look at myself.

But Grandma radiated pride. "You are so beautiful, just look."

I didn't want to.

I was terrified for some reason.

130

Grandma scooched me to a mirror against my will, and my breath caught in my throat.

The dress.

Me.

I . . .

A swirling galaxy wrapped around my body as if I were the sun in its center.

I did it.

I had brought my imagination to life.

And now I was going to show it to the people who held my future in their hands. The judges who would decide whether or not my dreams came true. All of it rested on this dress.

And it was spectacular.

Grandma kissed my cheek. "Now get up there and show them how talented you are."

Back to reality.

Back to my entire nervous system shutting down.

There was so much pressure on this moment, on this runway. My entire future depended on it.

I nearly swallowed my tongue when the announcer said, "Jeraline Arnold!"

"That's you, go!" Grandma gently shoved me forward.

Scrambling up the stairway, I walked up onto the start of the runway.

I couldn't believe I was doing this.

Puke.

Yup.

Gonna puke.

The woman in charge of the models waved frantically for me

to go. Charged up with nerves and terror, I stepped out onto the runway and tried to walk "cool" without flailing like a total idiot.

My eyes met Josh's, and my stomach twisted in on itself, but I managed a small smile. He gave me a little wave and a grin. Did I feel calmer or more nervous? I couldn't tell. In fact, I wasn't even sure if I had circulation in my legs.

The judges sat behind their table, stern faces, marking their papers, watching my every move.

Why did I do this on purpose?

Grandma was now in the front row with Buster, and she motioned for me to smile.

Right. Smile. As opposed to what I had probably been doing, which was a lot of grimaces and horror-stricken widened eyeballs.

I sure hoped my plastered grin didn't make me look like a serial killer, but it was all I had in me at the moment.

I couldn't do this.

I wanted to run.

I wanted to hide.

My legs grew more and more numb, and I didn't think I'd make it down the runway.

I moved as if the air was made from invisible mud, slow and out of place.

Another model walked toward me, going at normal speed, stomping fiercely.

As she marched closer, her entire body transformed into my attacker from the alley.

I shook my head to snap out of it, but nothing functioned properly. The model kept coming toward me, her face still my attacker's.

I turned to the audience in hopes to break myself out of this nightmare, to see Josh, Grandma, or Buster.

I stopped breathing as every single face in the building was now my attacker's.

Legs stopped working.

The model with the attacker's face stomped on a direct course toward me, five feet away, four, three, two, one . . .

In a panic, I moved to the right to avoid a collision when I should have moved left. The model lost her balance.

Still wearing my attacker's face, the model used my dress to break her fall.

With a loud *rip*, the bottom half of my dress detached itself from the bodice.

Time slowed down as if to force me to remember every second of humiliation.

Beads popped off the dress, flying in every direction, tumbling onto the runway and into the audience.

Clanking and pattering on the floor, it sounded like rain on a tin roof.

The strangest thought pounded in my head as the beads I'd so painstakingly sewn on fell into the audience: I had caused this. By crying on my dress, I'd created these tears that were now pouring onto the floor.

They were my tears come to life, held in so tightly that they had broken free.

To make me face what I had done to that man.

It was penance.

I stood rock still.

Everyone's faces were back to normal as my embarrassment

133

brought me back to reality.

My eyes met Josh's, agony threatening to make me lose consciousness, but I still stood there on the runway, frozen in my bodice and underwear, the petticoat and skirt of the universe at my feet.

The audience gasped as a whole, wrenching sympathy in every single expression.

Fight or flight.

Full panic now.

Flight.

Yanking up my petticoat and the bottom half of my dress up to my waist, I ran off the stage.

A blurred Josh tried to stop me, but I ran past him toward the exit. At least I was close to home.

"Jeraline!" I heard his voice, but I didn't stop.

I ran all the way home, nearly tripping up the stairs from the amount of fabric I held in my hands and arms. Racing inside the apartment, I let the skirt fall to the ground so that all I wore was a bodice and elastic-waisted petticoat.

Shame, terror, rage, sadness pushed down on my chest, making it difficult to take in air. I ran into my room and slammed the cutting table against the wall in anger, hearing the snaps of the metal legs as they bent in ways they weren't supposed to.

It wasn't enough.

I still hurt.

I threw my sewing machine off my desk, my hands shaking violently now.

I needed to stop.

I needed to breathe.

I needed to calm down.

I needed to cry.

Falling on the chair, I put my head down on the now empty desk and sobbed. Everything that had happened to me, that I had done, washed through me and came out in tears, forming small pools on the desk's surface.

A hand on my shoulder.

I turned to see Olivia, her child's face watching me with sympathy. "It wasn't that bad."

The only answer I gave was a choking sob.

She stayed like that for a while, her hand on my shoulder while I cried. "This isn't just about the runway show, is it?"

I shook my head, my insides twisting further at everything I had experienced: my parents being killed, the gun, the attack, the echoes of gunfire. Grandma was gone.

I was alone.

But it *was* about the show as well. It had been my hope, my salvation, my way out. Now it was gone. "I really, really lost, didn't I?"

Olivia tried to make me feel better. "You have no idea how they'll judge this contest. The runway show was probably for fun or publicity."

"Well, I gave them some good publicity," I cried. Taking a deep breath, I slowly began to calm myself, to regain some kind of composure. "I'm losing it." Then I thudded my head back on my desk, dramatically. "And Josh was there."

Olivia nodded in understanding. "Everyone has a moment like that once in their life."

"I just seem to have more of them." My tears dried up, and I

135

was left with an aching stillness.

Olivia stared at me with genuine concern but was apparently at a loss for words.

"What am I going to do?" I asked, knowing she couldn't give me any answers.

She disappeared, and I was left sitting at my desk, staring at my sewing machine and broken table on the floor.

No, really.

What was I going to do?

THE RETURN OF THE STOLEN PICTURE
(Yup, it's exactly what you think.)

The Hidden Corner sign loomed before me like a harbinger of the horrors to come. I didn't want to work today. I'd have to face Josh. He'd seen me in my underwear! So did a hundred other complete strangers, but Josh?

It hurt.

A lot.

Not even the gigantic plaster book spines cheered me up this morning, because the thought of walking in there and seeing Josh's pity for me was too much to bear.

I should just quit.

No.

I lived by myself now. I needed to pay the bills. And I needed to return Josh's photo.

What if I got caught? That thought was more humiliating than having my skivvies displayed to an entire warehouse full of people.

I had reached the front door. Time to get this over with.

Walking in, I immediately saw Josh at the cash register.

Look away. Look away. Look away.

"Hey there." His voice carried over the rant inside my head.

I chose to ignore him completely and hurry to the back room. Once there, I plopped my backpack in the locker and was about to take out the stolen picture of Josh when I completely chickened out and zipped my bag shut. Stuffing the backpack into the locker, I shut it. Maybe I could take it out later.

I might as well tackle the current issue full-on though, so I joined Josh behind the counter at the second register.

I felt his stare, but I didn't look at him.

"You were great yesterday."

Excuse me? Was that some kind of joke? I whirled to face him, to see if there was any sarcasm or teasing involved, but his eyebrows were all crinkled with concern.

Yup.

Pity.

He continued, "I think you'll win anyway. If that girl hadn't tripped . . ."

"Let's not relive it, please." That sounded harsh. But I couldn't listen to a play-by-play of the disaster that was yesterday.

"Sorry." Josh lowered his eyes, seemingly mortified at causing me any more pain.

"It's okay."

And the strangest thing happened.

The whole incident suddenly became funny.

I smiled. "At least they won't forget me."

Josh smiled back.

There was a giddy rush between us.

"Would you like to have dinner with me sometime?" Josh asked.

"What?" Was this real? Did he actually ask me that?

"Dinner. Tomorrow night?" Josh appeared hopeful.

Hopeful.

For me.

To say yes.

"I . . . uh . . . yeah, sure." He *for sure* knew I liked him now. Yup.

"If you don't want to, it's okay. I don't want to make you uncomfortable." Josh backed up a step, unsure.

Fix this!

"No, I'd love to." The words rushed out.

Josh's shoulders relaxed with what I could only describe as relief. Relief! Relief that I had said yes!

"Good. I'll pick you up at five." Josh smiled.

I was sure I was about to say or do something completely embarrassing that would change Josh's whole stance on wanting to have dinner with me, but I was saved by Rachel when she arrived at the counter and said, "Jeraline, can I talk to you in the back room?"

Not ominous at all.

"Of course." I swallowed hard.

I smiled briefly at Josh as I left the counter and followed Rachel to the back room.

Once inside, there was an awkward chunk of time where Rachel stood there staring at me, as if she was unsure what to say.

Oh man.

She was going to fire me.

I was too weird even for her. Too awkward. Too something.

Finally, she spoke. "I heard about what happened yesterday . . ."

Another awkward lapse of time as Rachel searched for what to say.

What had she heard? Who had told her? Why did she care?

"Maybe if you had made the dress stronger—"

No.

This was the very last thing on the planet I needed to hear right now. Was she honestly trying to make me feel worse? Was she that evil?

I interrupted her before she finished. "Just stop. Yesterday was hard enough as it was."

And she stopped. Her eyes expressed that she understood completely. Dare I say it, she looked apologetic?

"I'm sorry. I can't seem to stop myself with you. I honestly don't know why—"

"I don't want to talk about yesterday with you." Bold. I had been bold. So unlike me.

Straightening her outfit as if putting up an invisible wall between us, she pushed forward. "Well, too bad, because . . . I wanted to tell you that I'm proud of you for trying. It takes a lot of guts to do what you did, and no matter what happened, you should be proud of yourself for doing it."

Huh?

I stood there in mute shock, and before I responded, Rachel swung around and walked out of the back room, leaving me to ponder what had just happened.

Edmond materialized next to the locker with an expression of surprise. "Well, that was unexpected."

I barely nodded. I was still a little shocked. "That was almost . . . nice."

"Maybe you were right. Maybe there is a decent person in there somewhere." Edmond motioned to the locker next to him. "What do you say? Time to return the picture? She might not fire you after all."

He disappeared as I opened the locker and pulled out Josh's picture from my backpack.

Josh. Walked. In.

"Hey, you okay?" he asked.

Then he saw it.

The picture.

Me.

Holding the stolen picture.

"I . . ." What could I say?

"Is that the picture that was stolen?" Josh appeared genuinely confused.

It was all too much.

Dropping the picture to the ground, I grabbed my backpack and ran out the door.

"Jeraline!" Josh's voice followed me out, but I ignored it. I didn't stop. I couldn't stop.

In tears, I raced through the store, the front exit seemingly miles away.

Every few feet my attacker from the alley appeared, blood gushing down his face, until I was pushing my way through hundreds of him. Finally, I busted out and reached the front door, leaving the store.

I didn't stop there. My feet kept pounding the pavement, running, running from everything, running from my life.

I stopped cold when I reached the alley.

The alley was the root of it all. The physical embodiment of everything wrong with my life. It kept pushing me down, taking away any progress I'd made. Death, guns, brutality, darkness, and fear. I had to face it. It was the only way to defeat it. It was the only way I could live.

I plunged into the center of the alley, swallowed whole.

Noises jumped out at every corner, whispering to me that I didn't belong there, that I'd be consumed and devoured if I stayed a second longer.

Everything began to spin around me, and a shadowy figure approached me, gun in hand. He began to take form, but instead of my attacker, it was the young shooter that had killed my parents.

Gunshots and screams blasted all around the alley, coming from nowhere and everywhere all at once.

Then I saw them.

My parents.

Lying dead at my feet, blood soaking through their clothes and covering my shoes.

Squeezing my eyes shut, I slammed my hands over my ears to make everything go away.

It didn't.

The noises overpowered my measly attempt to block them.

Barking, growling, screaming, gunfire.

I opened my eyes, the darkness closing in on me like black fog.

I had to get out.

I had tried to defeat it, but I failed.

It was too powerful.

So I ran.

Ran out of the darkness and back on the sidewalk where I was out of its reach.

The alley had won.

I had lost.

After racing the rest of the way home, I flew up the stairs and swung the front door wide, leaping into the apartment. My safety zone. Almost as if nothing could touch me here, though I knew that wasn't true.

Entering my room, I slammed the door shut behind me even though I lived alone . . . habit. Sitting on the floor by my bed, I pulled out the gun from underneath it. As I held back tears, my hands fumbled along the surface of the revolver, and I began to hyperventilate. I dropped the gun back in the box and slid it under the bed.

I didn't ever want to see it again.

Reaching up to my bedside table, I yanked the picture of my parents down and into my lap, tracing their faces with my finger. "You must be so disappointed in me."

My mother stared up at me from the Empire State Building, tears in her eyes. "Jeraline, we love you. You could never disappoint us."

"But I shot someone. I did what was done to you. I'm evil," I cried.

Dad held Mom's hand tight as he looked up at me as well. "You are not evil. You did what you had to do to survive."

"That's just an excuse! I'm making you say things I want to hear! You're not here!" I threw the picture across the room, and the glass shattered as it hit the wall.

Everything was falling apart.

I was falling apart.

I jumped when my cell phone rang in my pocket. It was so surprising, I didn't check to see who it was before I pulled it out and answered, "Hello?"

"Jeraline?" It was Rachel.

Yup.

The firing.

I sighed, knowing full well where this conversation was going. "Hi, Rachel. You don't have to tell me. I know I'm fired."

There was a pause, then her voice actually sounded . . . concerned? "No . . . I . . . wanted to make sure you're okay."

Huh?

"But I stole the picture."

"Well, I knew you did that a long time ago. I have security cameras and I live here, remember?"

Gulp.

"Then why . . . ?" I couldn't fathom how she hadn't fired me yet if she had known all along.

"I wanted you to admit it," Rachel said matter-of-factly. Then I swear she smirked when she continued, "And you did."

"Oh." For someone who loved books, I was certainly full of words.

"Anyway, I should have called you this morning to give

you some time off. After yesterday, you need to recover and decompress, but by no means are you fired." Then she paused, and when she spoke again, her tone was thoughtful and kind. "You love these books almost more than I do."

I paused.

She paused.

A warmth carried through the phone.

Were we bonding? Did I like her?

Then reality set in. "How am I going to face Josh?"

Rachel sighed. "He'll get over it. He should take it as a compliment." Then her voice went back to what I was used to, stern and commanding. "I'll expect you on Monday." Without another word, Rachel hung up.

I stared at my cell phone both relieved and bewildered.

What just happened?

Then, eyeing the broken glass in front of me, I carefully reached over and lifted the picture of my parents, gently brushing off any excess shards. "Sorry, for throwing you."

Mom turned to me, shaking her head. "Clean up that mess before you cut yourself."

Shrugging, I stood up.

Delusion or not, she was right.

Time to go get the vacuum cleaner.

ROOFING AND SPECIAL GUEST STARS
(I'm still trying to recover.)

Exhausted didn't cover what I was experiencing one iota. Squeezing my hands into a fist was a monumental effort at this point and not just because I wore thick leather protective gloves. Not to mention the sun beating down on my back and neck. The hard hat kept my head safe from sunburns, but not even its bright white color reflected the heat enough to prevent my entire scalp from sweating profusely. Yup. Dripping in my eyes now.

Roofing was hard.

So far, my main task was scraping off the old shingles. Buster had given me a quick tutorial and handed me a tool called a "tear-off bar," and its purpose was written right in the title. Basically, it was the same shape as a shovel, but a flatter surface at the bottom, with sharp teeth for digging underneath those shingles and popping them off. I had to admit it was pretty satisfying when I'd scoop up a giant clump of roof instead of the three or four shingles at a time that was more the norm, for me, anyway. At least the roof was flat-ish, only a slight incline, which did make it easier to stand and move around without fear of tumbling to my death (this was a still a worry of course, because . . . me), but it did take some of the anxiety away.

One more patch left. Then done. With the scraping at least. There was still the whole roof to be reshingled. But Buster was on it. He'd clear the areas I deshingled by using a handy-dandy magnetic nail sweeper that acted like a broom with a magnet as the sweeper. Then he laid down the roofing paper and placed the new shingles down, using a roof nailer to secure them in place.

It was all very efficient, but also very tiring.

The upside was getting to know Buster a little more. He was a fascinating guy full of stories. From his days as a roofer and dealing with some very eccentric clients, to being a part of a theater troop in Korea (the stories of the food alone made me want to go), to his first wife, who had died around the same time Gramps had; it all added up to a life fully lived with no regrets.

But most of all he was funny, which made me happy since my grandmother's favorite thing to do was laugh. I could still remember watching the original *Pink Panther* and her laughing so hard she fell off the couch. Some of Buster's quips had brought tears to my eyes they were so funny. With everything that had happened in the last few days, I needed it. And he knew I needed it, which was why he put in the extra effort. It made me love him just a little bit.

Roofing also brought back memories of my dad. We'd only repaired a half dozen houses over the years, but it was the time we spent together that I remembered most. Sitting on the rooftop after a long day's work, eating peanut butter and jelly sandwiches Mom made for us with the crusts cut off and drinking an ice-cold soda. My face flushed with the memory, and the old familiar ache crawled back inside my chest.

Shingles.

Almost done.

Concentrate.

After I tossed the last of the old shingles off the roof, Grandma walked out from the house, holding a tray with two large glasses on it. "I made you two some lemonade."

Better words were never spoken.

Buster wiped the sweat off his brow with his sleeve. "Our savior."

"You are the best. We'll be right down." Unclamping my hands from the tear-off bar, I took a deep breath heading for the ladder.

"Jeraline?"

Was that . . .

Josh?

I whirled around to see where the voice had come from.

It wasn't Josh.

It was *my attacker* standing on Buster's front lawn, and he was pulling out a gun!

I jumped in spite of myself and slipped on the newly installed roofing paper. Regaining my balance didn't seem to be an option as I slid off the roof and fell all thirteen feet to land directly onto . . .

Josh.

Yup. Not my attacker. Josh.

The brunt force of my landing pushed Josh to the ground so that I was now lying on top of him with his arms around me.

"Did you hit your head? Are you okay?" I asked frantically, afraid I had given him a concussion.

"Am I okay? Are you okay? You fell off a roof." Josh stated the obvious, but for some reason it made what happened moments ago click in my brain.

I had fallen off the roof.

And I was in Josh's arms.

"Are you both okay?" Buster was halfway down the ladder with terror.

Grandma had abandoned the lemonade tray and raced to our side.

I scrambled to my feet and helped Josh up with my hand, then pulled off my hard hat.

"I'm absolutely fine," Josh kept repeating as Grandma inspected him thoroughly, to my horror.

"Let me check you both. I can't believe you fell off the roof. I've been worried about Buster falling all day, and it end up being my twenty-two-year-old granddaughter?" Grandma fussed.

"Grandma, I'm fine, I promise." I tried to placate her, but her worry-face was strong at the moment. Turning to Josh, I asked again, "Are you sure you're okay? I didn't hurt you?"

"I'm a hundred percent fine. I didn't mean to scare you like that. I'm just glad I was here to break your fall," Josh tried to joke.

Then it really hit me.

Josh was here.

Standing on Buster's front lawn.

And before I could stop myself, I asked more bluntly than I

149

intended, "What are you doing here?"

But Josh didn't take offense. He smiled at me as if I should know something I obviously didn't. "It's Saturday, remember?"

Saturday?

Oh, dinner.

Our date.

Grandma, apparently, had finished her health inspection of us both as Buster arrived at our side. "I'm Anna by the way, Jeraline's grandmother, and this beautiful man right here is Buster."

Josh shook both their hands with a grin. "Josh."

"Oh, I know who you are. You were at the runway show supporting Jeraline. We didn't get to meet considering what happened . . ." Grandma side-eyed me with a big "oops."

"Grandma," I groaned. The last thing I wanted to talk about was the runway show.

Grandma got the hint as she nodded toward the porch and the abandoned lemonade tray. "I made some lemonade. Why don't you two catch up on the porch." She discreetly winked at me as she kissed Buster on the cheek.

Buster also gave me a conspiratorial raise of an eyebrow, then nodded at Josh. "Good to meet you. If you two don't mind, I need a bit of shade. Anna and I will drink our lemonade inside."

With another thinking-they're-clever smile between Grandma and Buster, I tried desperately not to die of embarrassment as they entered the house.

Now I was alone.

With Josh.

Turning back to him, I tried to regain my bearings. "I thought after what happened . . . you wouldn't want to see me."

"I followed you here this morning. I've been psyching myself up to come and talk to you for the last four hours. What you did was very sweet. I'm sorry I didn't go after you to tell you that."

My brain couldn't form words.

Was this a fantasy?

From the awkward shift of Josh's position, I knew it wasn't. "You could say something."

Did he really think speaking was that easy?

"I . . . need some lemonade. Let's go sit?" That was me: such a player.

But Josh nodded with a half-turned smile and an ease to his steps as we walked up the three stairs of Buster's porch. Sitting on the swing-bench with the two glasses of lemonade that Grandma left, Josh lazily rocked the swing with his foot.

After taking a large, relieving gulp, I began to feel human again.

Sipping on his glass, Josh asked, "Where'd you learn to roof?"

"That's all Buster. Apparently, he worked for a roofing company for years. And my dad was kind of a handyman, doing odd jobs here and there, so he repaired a couple of roofs and I'd help. It's weird how it all comes back to you though. It's kind of nice, keeps me distracted from . . . my life."

"Is it that bad?"

The echo of the gunshot rang in my ear as I pulled the trigger on my attacker. "Why *did* you come? I mean, I'm glad you did, but why?"

Josh shifted on the bench, causing it to sway crooked. "Do you think I'm just a guy who's so into himself I couldn't possibly like anyone?"

"No, I didn't mean it like that."

"Do you think that little of yourself?"

Ouch.

And yes.

"I'm saying everything wrong." I hated all words that came out of my mouth.

"You don't know me." Josh's tone was sad, as if he wanted to change that.

"You don't know me either." Why am I me?

But Josh smiled ruefully. "And that's why I came."

I smiled back, and a moment passed between us. A good moment. A comfortable moment.

But then I had to speak again. "Don't you ever feel that if you start to show your true self, people will run away screaming?" I *was* scared of what people would think of me. The true me. The one who played out her nightmares in real time.

Josh leaned back on the swing, and we rocked slowly as the sun moved closer to the horizon. "I can't imagine running away from you ever."

I killed someone.

"Nothing could be that bad," Josh added lightly.

I killed someone.

"Hypothetically, being a murderer would be pretty bad." How do I live with that?

"You're talking about killing someone?" Josh reared his head back and chuckled. "I think that should be the least of your worries, Jeraline."

But it happened.

I killed someone.

"Trust me. You're not the murdering type."

I am though.

I did it.

It happened.

"What's the murdering type? Buster? He killed men in war." Why was I going down this road? Why with Josh? I didn't know his favorite color, for goodness sake.

"That's different." Josh kept the bench rocking with his foot.

"How is it different? He still has to live with it." Tell me. Tell me how it was different.

"It was him or them." Josh shrugged as if this explained everything.

"But it'll be with Buster forever. I don't see how it could ever fade," I said desperately. Would it? Would it ever fade? Even though it was self-defense?

Steadying the bench with his foot, he turned to me with a thoughtful expression on his face. "It's just something that happens I guess. It's not fair, but you learn to live with it, and it becomes a part of you."

Nodding, I began to push the bench with my foot. "I'm tired of being scared of everything."

"Are you scared of me?" Josh's eyes shifted nervously, expectant.

Duh.

"A little," I admitted.

Josh reached over, and his lips met mine. It was tentative at first, but when I began to kiss him back, it became more assured, then I forgot everything else because my mind went completely blank from my brain exploding.

153

Pulling away felt like yanking a rip cord that happened to be my nervous system.

Josh held my cheek in his hand, our faces inches from each other. "At least I'm one less thing to be fearful of."

I wasn't so sure about that.

The sky had turned a glowing purplish red as the sun slowly lowered past the houses across from us on the horizon.

"I have a question for you." Josh watched me as if he was gauging my reaction.

Uh-oh.

"Yes?"

"Why did you take my picture?"

And I found the question didn't scare me as much as I thought it would. "I don't know anymore. I thought I needed it at the time."

Josh pulled out his cell phone and showed me a picture of the two of us at the counter in the store.

"Where did you get that?" I asked, wondering why he'd have a picture of me that he didn't delete.

"It was a shot of the front room for the website. Rachel sent it to me. She wanted to cut you out of it, but I cropped it so it was just you and me. I guess I needed it at the time too."

Oh.

Really?

My face flushed.

Josh liked me. As in, I wasn't a lone crazy person in this situation.

Taking another sip of his lemonade, Josh asked, "What about your dress from the competition? Please tell me you kept it."

"It now lies in a pile on my bedroom floor, but yes."

"You should fix it. You're beautiful in it."

My brain sizzled in response. Another explosion was imminent.

Leaning down a second time, Josh kissed me again. This time I wasn't as scared. It felt as if we were destined to kiss each other. My mind went fuzzy again as his lips pressed against mine.

Pulling away, Josh positioned himself so that I could lean on his chest. "So? Hungry?"

"Extremely."

Kissing the top of my head, Josh said, "Let's get some dinner."

I sighed in happiness.

"Okay."

HANK!
(I'm the worst person ever!)

Entering my apartment, I couldn't stop smiling.

The night had been perfect.

I tossed my backpack on the couch and stretched out my sore muscles.

Josh kissed me!

And we had a lovely dinner of peanut butter and jelly sandwiches with the crusts cut off furnished by Grams. She had obviously remembered my favorite "work" meal I used to have with Dad as well. It made me love her more, if that was even possible.

Replaying every word of every part of the conversations Josh and I had together tonight, I was relieved that only a couple sentences would haunt me for the rest of my days. That was nothing for me! I did pretty good. And what was crazier was that I actually wanted to see him again. I didn't want to hide under the bed and never come out.

Progress.

I was about to go into my bedroom and call it a night when I glanced over to the kitchen counter and saw the plate of cookies Grandma had made a few days ago.

My stomach dropped.

Hank!

I had told him to wait for me Friday to give him dinner, but I had stormed out after getting caught with Josh's stolen picture. His dinner and my lunch were both still in the fridge.

I knew I wasn't his keeper, and I knew he didn't rely only on me for food, but I had promised.

The thought of Hank standing there by the dumpster waiting for me? My stomach curdled in pain at the thought.

Maybe he was around. I had to try.

Shoving the entire plate of cookies into a bag and rummaging through the refrigerator for anything I could find, I finally left my apartment with three paper lunch bags full of food.

Though my body was exhausted from a day of hard labor, I ran. Ran past the alley, ran past all the buildings, and ran past the front of the bookstore, cleared the corner, until I stood panting next to the dumpster.

Rachel lived upstairs, and I didn't want to wake her, so I whispered as loudly as I could, "Hank! Are you here?"

Darkness blocked almost all light. Not even the streetlamp a few yards away was enough to see anything clearly, but I searched all the same. Maybe he was sleeping nearby? Maybe he was leaned up against the wall?

Maybe he was nowhere near here.

Giving up wasn't an option though.

"Hank!" I whispered louder. "I have some food for you." I may have overcompensated with the three paper bags, but at least he'd have food for a while. If I could find him.

But nothing.

No sound. No voice. No ruffling.

Hank wasn't here.

"Jeraline? Is that you?" Rachel's voice sounded from above my head.

Uh-oh.

Guess I was too loud.

Rachel poked her head out of the upstairs window with what I could only describe as a snarl.

"Hey, Rachel." Very professional.

"What are you doing down there?" she grumbled. Yes, she actually grumbled.

"I . . . it's . . . there's this really nice homeless guy Hank that I give food to when I work, and well . . . I forgot yesterday when I . . . left." Articulate, powerful, moving.

"Well, he doesn't seem to be here now, and you're waking up the entire street. Go home."

Hey, she didn't fire me.

Holding three brown paper bags, standing in the dark, with my boss yelling at me from a second story window. Not my finest moment.

Wait.

A moaning sound, very faint, and possibly in my imagination.

"Hank?" I whispered so as not to anger any of Rachel's supposed neighbors.

And there it was again. But this time I heard Hank's voice. It was muffled and sounded far away. "Jeraline? Is that you?"

I searched everywhere around the dumpster, behind it, near it, but I couldn't figure out where Hank's voice had come from.

"Hank, where are you?" I whispered desperately, panic setting in.

There was a brief pause as I waited.

"Well? Is he there?" Rachel seemed to be on pins and needles as well.

"I can't find him anywhere!" Breathe. You'll find him. Breathe.

"I'm in the dumpster." Hank projected his voice loud enough for me to hear.

I threw the lid up, leaning it against the building wall, then looked inside: garbage everywhere. Still too dark to see.

Cell phone.

I pulled the cell phone out from my back pocket and turned on the flashlight. Why I hadn't thought of this sooner was beyond me.

Rachel called out to me from above, "What's happening? Is he in there?"

"I think so. Hang on," I answered.

As I flashed the light around the inside of the dumpster, Hank's head was visible, though his body was buried in trash.

"Jeraline, I'm stuck," Hank groaned.

"What happened?" My shoulders both untensed and tensed at the sight of Hank. On one hand, I was relieved to find him, but on the other . . . dumpster.

"I climbed in like a young fool. They all make dumpster diving look so easy. I think I broke my ankle. These fumes are killing me. I've been here over a day," he confessed.

159

"Hank!"

I couldn't climb in fast enough, my guilt guiding me. I landed my feet gently on the garbage, careful not to step where Hank's body might be.

But once I was there . . .

The smell.

I retched, though nothing came out. I imagined what Hank had gone through having lain in the bottom of this cesspool for the last day, and my stomach twisted in sympathy.

And another problem.

I wasn't strong enough to lift a full-grown man out of a dumpster. I needed help.

Calling up to Rachel, I said, "Call an ambulance and get down here and help me. I can't lift him out of here alone."

In the darkness I saw the whites of Rachel's eyes widen in terror. "I'll call the ambulance, but we should wait for them to move him."

Right.

Afraid to leave her house.

It was always a theory, but now, from the horrified expression on her face, I knew it was true. But I couldn't pull out Hank alone. I wasn't physically capable. I needed to convince her.

"Rachel, I need you," I said sternly, hoping she'd overcome her fear and race down to help.

But she simply stared at me with frightened eyes.

"Please," I begged, though I knew I was arguing with someone's deep-rooted phobia, and I wasn't sure if a simple please would work.

I had to try alone. There was no other choice.

Turning to Hank, I kept my voice calm. "I'm going to try and dig you out of here."

Clumps of wet paper, plastics, and rotted food all covered Hank with a dense thickness that stuck to my hands when I peeled the layers away. Hank's hand appeared as he managed to shove some of the garbage aside as well. I used it as a beacon and slopped off clumps of decay until his arm was free.

The stench caused me to gag once more, but thankfully no vomit. Just what this dumpster needed: another foul-smelling ingredient to add to its disgusting soup.

"Why didn't you call for help?" I asked Hank as we both managed to free his second arm.

"I did. No one heard me. I thought I was going to die here." Hank's breath was ragged and fast.

My worry, concern, and guilt motivated me further as I leaned down and placed Hank's arm over my shoulder. "I'm so sorry I wasn't here."

"It's not your fault. I'm the sixty-year-old idiot who climbed in here." Hank positioned his arm so that I could pull him up.

"You're not an idiot. You were hungry." Because I forgot to give you food. My fault. My fault. Sandwiching my feet solidly on the garbage, I squatted into position. "We're going to try and get you to stand on three . . . One, two, three."

We moved a few feet up, then my foot shifted from the unstable garbage, and we both fell back down. This time I was also lying on the bed of filth.

"Maybe we should wait for the paramedics." I began to see the intelligence in Rachel's idea.

Hank shifted his arm so he sat up a bit more, then stared

down at me, serious. "If the boss lady told them I was a bum, they're not coming, or they're not coming for a while anyway. They have more important people to save."

No.

My hands shook with rage and determination. "You are just as important. We're doing this." Pushing myself up, I stabilized my feet once more on the precarious garbage flow.

One last glance up at Rachel's window to ask for help, but it was closed. She'd given up on us, expecting the paramedics to do their job.

"It's just you and me, Hank. We got this." Our eyes met, and we both understood each other. I would get him out of this dumpster or die trying.

A touch on my arm, and it wasn't Hank.

Rachel stood there, her shaking hand now bracing my arm, eyes pried open from terror. "I'm here. I'm helping." Her voice quavered, and her breathing was hard despite the wretched smell.

Placing my hand on hers, I forced her to make eye contact with me. "We'll get you back inside as soon as we help Hank, okay?"

Rachel's breath was fast and panicked, but she nodded in agreement. "Let's get this over with."

I'd take it.

She threw her leg over the side of the dumpster, and I helped her the rest of the way inside. Her hands continued to shake, and I was sure we were finally going to add some puke to the mix, but not yet anyway.

We positioned ourselves on either side of Hank while he placed one arm on each of our shoulders.

"Ready?" I asked.

They nodded.

"Now."

With a large, unified grunt, we lifted Hank to his feet. As soon as his feet had pressure on them, he groaned in pain. "Yup, it's twisted, maybe broken."

"We gotta get you out of here so we can get a better look." I honestly wasn't sure what kind of assessment I'd be able to make, as I knew absolutely nothing about injuries, but I did know we all needed out of this rot pit.

Shifting an inch at a time, we finally faced the long edge of the dumpster.

It was so high.

"How do we get him over *that* with a bum ankle?" Rachel asked what we were all thinking.

"I'll catch him from the other side." I had no idea if this would work, but what else could we do? Quickly hopping out of the dumpster, I grabbed both Hank's forearms. "You're going to have to roll out and use me as support. Which ankle is it? I'll make sure you don't land on it."

Hank nodded in agreement. "It's the left one."

As I pulled Hank's front half over the lip of the dumpster, Rachel lifted Hank's legs carefully, and he used his stomach to roll over the edge. His weight shifted as he leaned toward my side, so I moved and grabbed his middle, allowing Hank to put his right leg down first.

And he was out.

Rachel climbed out almost instantaneously and paused, unsure if she should do more, so I let her off the hook. "You can go back inside. I'll wait with Hank for the ambulance."

Rachel's fear took over, and she hurried to the open door, but instead of closing it, she stayed in the doorway, safe inside but still part of the action.

Surprisingly, it didn't take long for the ambulance to arrive—one for the good guys. Hank shifted on his good foot uncomfortably at the sight of the two paramedics hurrying over.

The closest paramedic's nostrils flared at our smell, but then his face turned all business. "I'm Jim, and this is Lucy."

"Nice to meet you. I'm Jeraline. This is Hank, the patient, and that's Rachel. She owns this place," I said, not knowing what else to say. Then I explained, "Sorry about the smell. He got stuck in the dumpster. His ankle might be broken."

Lucy didn't seem fazed by the stink, and at seeing Hank's condition, Jim lost his concern for the stench as he examined Hank's ankle. When Hank moaned in pain at Jim's touch, Jim assessed, "It doesn't feel broken, but he'll need an X-ray to be sure."

Hank stuttered, "I . . . don't have any money."

Lucy pulled out a portable gurney from the ambulance and wheeled it over. "That's the hospital's problem. We're going to get you in and make sure they get you an X-ray." Lucy clenched her jaw with determination, and I'd bet Hank wasn't the first homeless person she'd fought for.

I liked her.

And so did Hank, as he managed a smile through pain-gritted teeth.

Jim and Lucy helped Hank lie down on the gurney, while I held his hand.

"You going to be okay?" I asked, both of us covered in filth.

Hank squeezed my hand. "I am now. Thank you, Jeraline. I owe you."

"Where are you going to stay the night?" My mind raced, imagining the hospital kicking him out after the X-ray.

"Don't worry about me. The shelter I stay at sometimes is close to the hospital," Hank assured me.

Lucy's eyes solidly met mine. "I know the place. We'll make sure he gets there."

Before Hank let go of my hand, he nodded toward the dumpster. "You probably couldn't see it in the dark, but I finished your painting. It's leaning up against the side of the dumpster."

"Hank." My chest tightened. He'd come for food and to give me my painting, and I hadn't been here.

But he didn't act upset at all. He squeezed my hand one more time. "I'll see you soon, Jeraline."

"Bye, Hank." I let go of his hand as Lucy and Jim situated Hank into the ambulance and sped off toward the hospital.

Flashlight beaming on my phone again, I walked over to the side of the dumpster, and next to my abandoned lunch bags was the most stunning painting I'd ever seen.

Even with the poor lighting of the flashlight, it took my breath away.

Swirling colors of paint swam together in a beautiful dance to create a perfect snapshot of the Milky Way. Though the canvas was small, the imagery was so much larger. The more I stared, the more it felt as if I were swimming in the very universe itself.

Hank was a true artist.

Tears filled my eyes and fell down my cheeks.

"What is that?" Rachel's voice cut through the silence.

"It's a painting that Hank made for me." I tried to hide the choke in my voice.

Rachel's face softened, then she said, "Well, bring it and yourself inside, and let's get cleaned up."

I stared down at my stained and wet-with-garbage clothes with disgust.

Good plan.

WHO ARE YOU AND WHAT HAVE YOU DONE WITH RACHEL?
(Seriously.)

I sat on Rachel's couch, trying to relax after taking a scrub-down-oh-my-god-will-this-garbage-smell-ever-go-away shower, wearing a T-shirt and sweatpants from Rachel's wardrobe. I was trying to figure out what was more surreal, being stuck in a dumpster or being stuck in Rachel's apartment. Though, to be fair, Rachel had been nothing but kind to me since the whole debacle. I wondered what was going on in her brain since I figured it had been a while since she'd stepped outside. And, shocker, I was the one who made it a miserable experience. Her seething hate for me would come back at any moment, I just knew it. But for now, clean clothes and hot showers.

The sound of water pounding on the bathtub floor was the only noise that permeated the apartment. Rachel had been in the shower for a while now, like I had. She had let me go first, which again, was . . . nice. And she had even given me permission to stay in as long as I wanted since she had a tankless water heater installed a few months ago. It was almost as if the universe knew the two of us would be taking endless showers in the future.

Hank's painting lay in my lap, and I stared into its depths. Now that it was properly lit, I noticed so many more details. Layer upon layer of paint created a cacophony of stars, planets, debris, and infinite beauty. Staring into the center of the painting, it seemed endless, capturing eternity on a canvas.

My mind throbbed at the idea that all of Hank's other paintings had been discarded and destroyed.

So much lost.

Breathing in deep, I tried to calm myself. I set the painting down to rest against the arm of the couch.

Breathe.

With the painting out of sight, I decided to have a gander at Rachel's apartment. I mean, I had always wondered what this place looked like, and now here I was sitting in Rachel's living room, and I didn't know if I'd ever have another opportunity.

The floor space was as large as the store beneath us, which made it quite big for an apartment. Most of the square footage made up the living room/dining room/kitchen, but there were four doors scattered throughout, and I was only sure of two of them, one being the bathroom since I had taken the shower, and the other being Rachel's bedroom, from where she had brought out the clothes for me to wear. Walls were tastefully decorated with prints of famous paintings like *A Sunday Afternoon on the Island of La Grande Jatte*, which was the inspiration for the mural outside on the building of the bookstore. No wonder she was annoyed with me when I mentioned the Sondheim play. The painting had a place of honor above the couch I was currently sitting on. Tastefully decorated with neutral colors of tans, whites, and browns, I wasn't sure if this was how I imagined Rachel's place would look.

But the mantel was what caught my eye the most. Pictures. All of Rachel's son Kent. I recognized him from the photo I had found under the stacks. There must have been over thirty on her mantelpiece below the mounted flat-screen TV across from the couch. And now, seeing more photographs of Kent, it really was eerie how much he looked like Josh.

I was pulled out of my reverie when Rachel walked out of the bathroom, dressed in pajamas and pat-drying her hair with a towel.

"I'm sorry about tonight. Thank you so much for . . . everything," I stuttered.

Rachel sat on a chair next to me, placing the damp towel on the coffee table between us. "That was the first time in ten years I've left this building."

Whoa.

"Whoa." Apparently, I couldn't keep it in. I knew it was bad, but I hadn't been sure it was *that* bad.

"I kept thinking every day that I'd get out, for a walk, or the store, or anything, but I never did. Suddenly it's been a decade. It's terrifying, Jeraline, but the thought of leaving is even more terrifying." Rachel's eyes were round and frantic talking about it. Then she took a deep, calming breath and slightly chuckled. "Ten years of isolation, and I'm jumping in a dumpster helping some homeless guy."

"Hank. His name is Hank." I didn't know what compelled me to correct her, but hearing Hank being written off as simply "a homeless guy" hurt me. Our eyes both rested on Hank's painting.

"Yes, Hank." Motioning to the painting, Rachel asked, "May I?" Upon my nod of approval, she picked it up, examining its details. "Remarkable. I'm going to have to commission something from him when he's . . . healed up." After another moment of being lost in Hank's work, Rachel placed the painting back down next to me. "I'm sorry I've been so horrible to you."

"It's okay." It wasn't okay, but I couldn't seem to stop the people-pleaser in me.

"No, it really isn't. I just see you so scared of everything all the time, and I guess you remind me of *me*. And I don't like me very much," Rachel admitted.

And I knew. I knew that already. That was why I was able to stay for three years, because I knew there was no real hatred or malice behind her behavior. It was all about her, not about me. "You weren't wrong. I am scared of everything."

"But I am wrong. Look at what you did with the fashion show? You put yourself out there. That's a bigger win than you know right now at your age." She sighed, motioning to herself as if on display. "Trust me. I'm an agoraphobic forty-eight-year-old that pretends one of her employees is her dead son." She gestured to the slew of photos on the mantel.

Dead.

Oh.

"I'm sorry."

"He died in a car accident, and I haven't left this place since. Crazy, right?" Rachel's eyes searched mine, looking for something, some kind of response, but I wasn't sure what she wanted out of me.

I leaned back on the couch, thinking. "No. Not crazy at all. I've pretty much only been here and my apartment since my parents were killed a few years ago."

"Your parents were killed? I had no idea." Rachel reached over to the bottle of scotch on the coffee table and poured herself a drink. "Now I feel even worse." She motioned to the scotch. "You want one?"

I shook my head. Alcohol and I didn't mix so well.

Rachel took a sip of her drink, then leapt to her feet. "I know how I can make it up to you."

"Make it up to me? Uh, no, Rachel, I . . ."

But Rachel hurried into her bedroom, only to return a few seconds later with a book in her hands. Very purposefully, Rachel handed me the book.

A hardcover copy with the original sleeve of *The Gateway to Winterbrook*.

Um.

"Is this . . . ? How did you know . . . ? I can't . . ."

"It is. I overheard you and Josh. And you absolutely can." Rachel answered all of my questions.

The book. My Holy Grail. In my hands. I quickly opened it to the elusive golden page, and it was as beautiful as I'd imagined. Gold inlay of an intricately carved door was shiny and metallic despite being published over a hundred years ago. The door to Winterbrook. And given to me by . . . Rachel?

Rachel's face softened, and her eyes sparkled with genuine affection. "I used to read it to Kent when he was little. And hearing you say to Josh that your mom read it to you, and now I know she's gone . . ." Her eyes watered from emotion. "I sometimes imagine that Kent isn't really dead, that the rumors were true and that he escaped to Winterbrook through that page."

Tracing the golden pattern of the door with my finger, I found that I wished the same thing for my parents. That somehow the three of them had found each other and were living adventures in Winterbrook.

Breaking the momentary silence, Rachel said solemnly, "The book is yours. You were right. It was here in the bookstore the whole time, waiting for you."

Instantly my eyes welled up with tears as well.

"No tears. We'll both start sobbing, and as of two days ago I thought I didn't like you."

"Same," I answered before I thought about it.

We both cracked up at that.

"So you *did* name your store after the bookstore in *Winterbrook*?" I recalled how angry Rachel had been when I'd asked three years ago.

Slowly, she nodded.

I stared at the book in my hands and shook my head in awe. "Thank you. So much. This is . . . amazing."

"I can't argue with destiny." Rachel smiled, content.

Glancing at the time on my phone, I had a mini heart attack. "It's five a.m. I need to get home."

"You can crash on the couch. You shouldn't walk home this late. It's too dangerous."

I flinched from the sound of a gunshot.

My attacker hovered outside the second-story window, staring at me.

He disappeared.

"Are you okay?"

"Yeah, I'm good. I just need to get home. I'll be fine." I had to leave. I had to get out.

Rachel didn't push the argument. Our relationship was still fragile after all. "I'll walk you down."

"You don't have to do that."

"Yes, I do."

I got it. Things had changed. Rachel was different.

We were friends.

"Okay," I agreed.

I held both the painting and the book like the precious treasures they were, and we headed toward the door. It didn't take us long to walk down the stairs that led to the closed store. It was strange moving through the stacks in the dark with only Rachel. I'd done it many times before after closing, but it was different somehow.

Arriving at the front door, Rachel unlocked it for me and opened it.

I stepped outside and turned to Rachel.

It was time.

This time gently.

Carrying the painting and book in one hand, I reached out with my other hand, offering it to Rachel.

Terrified, Rachel shakily gave me her hand.

"You got this," I encouraged her.

Tears of fear rolled from Rachel's eyes, but she nodded, and slowly, inch by inch, she stepped out of the store. After a moment of truly being outside of her own free will, Rachel breathed in deep, forcing herself to calm down.

"You did it. You're here," I said quietly, worried I'd spook her.

Rachel tightened her grip on my hand. "Don't turn into me, Jeraline. Living in a constant state of fear isn't living." Her eyes searched mine for acknowledgment. "Promise me."

Her face morphed into my attacker's face, then quickly back again.

"I promise," I uttered, though it terrified me to do so.

Rachel patted my hand as if this was enough for her, then let me go.

"You going back in?" I asked her.

Peering up at the sky, Rachel stared as if it were for the first time. She shook her head with a small smile. "I think I'm going to stay out here for a while."

Without thinking, I hugged Rachel tightly. I needed to. I wanted to. And what shocked me more was that Rachel hugged me back just as fiercely.

"I'll see you at work," Rachel said kindly in my ear.

I pulled away, trying to hide the distance that crept up inside of me as I realized what I had to do. Waving the book gently, I said, "Thank you for the book."

"Of course," Rachel answered.

Leaving without another glance at Rachel, I started my trek home.

It was time.

I had to do it.

There was no other choice for me.

I had to turn myself in.

TIME TO FACE THE MUSIC
(Can I be someone else now please?)

I headed toward the alley one more time.

It didn't take long to get there and find what I was looking for: the Wanted poster for my attacker. The name had been ripped off, presumably years ago, but at least his face was clear. The first piece to my confession. I tore it from the brick, and it came off surprisingly easy, as if it were meant to be, because it *was* meant to be.

A deep resounding snicker boomed from the alley, and I tried to ignore it. It mocked me. It thought it had won the war. Maybe it had. But I didn't care anymore. I had to take responsibility for what I had done, and if that meant the alley had beaten me, then so be it.

My legs shook as I forced myself to walk back home to gather the last two items I'd need to own up to what I had done.

Trembling hands opened the door to my building, legs heavy as if made of stone climbed up the stairs, numb fingers placed the key in my front lock and turned the knob.

I reached my bedroom, placing Hank's painting on the bedside table and my book on the bed itself, then stuffed my attacker's wanted poster inside my backpack.

I collapsed to my knees, my body no longer able to support me.

Arms weighed down by terror pulled out the box holding the gun from under the bed. Lifting the revolver carefully, I placed it on my lap. I grabbed the shirt from under the mattress and shoved it into my backpack on top of the Wanted sign.

Why couldn't I do that with the gun?

Hank's painting began swirling into a black hole. I wished it would suck me into its vortex.

I knew what I had to do, yet I couldn't seem to move.

Olivia appeared, dangling her feet off the bed in front of me, gently holding the first edition of *The Gateway to Winterbrook* that Rachel had given me. "You finally got your prize, and now you're going to be locked up for years. I wonder if they'll let you bring the book?"

I didn't answer.

She wasn't real.

"You're doing the right thing," she continued, trying to get me to look at her.

"How can something feel so violently wrong and still be the right thing to do?" I asked, giving in to my imagination.

Olivia shrugged. "It's the way life is, I guess."

Not good enough.

"Maybe I should get rid of the gun and block the whole thing out of my memory. It could work." The words were empty. I knew I had to go. If only my legs would work.

Jumping off the bed, Olivia held her hand out for me to take.

I hesitated, not sure if I wanted to.

After a few long moments, I gently held her hand. Olivia bent her head down, forcing my eyes to meet hers until I was completely focused on her. "I'll go with you. I'll be your Marta. She saved me by helping me find myself again. Turning yourself in is the key. You know it. You feel it."

I did.

My legs moved.

I let go of Olivia's hand and grabbed my backpack, placing the gun inside, the last ingredient. Standing up, I threw the backpack over my shoulders and headed out the door.

One last thing.

Before I could chicken out, I pulled my cell phone out of my pocket and dialed.

"Hello?" Josh's voice sounded tired and groggy. (Probably because it was six in the morning.)

But I had to tell him.

I had to let him know I was a killer.

"Josh, it's Jeraline." My voice shook.

"Jeraline? It's so early. Is everything okay?"

"I shot someone."

"What?" He was awake now.

"I shot someone by the alley. I'm turning myself in." *You told him, now hang up.*

"Jeraline . . ."

"I thought you should know."

I hung up.

There. Done. Now he could move on. Not that he had much to move on from, but I'd never forget him.

I walked out of my room, my apartment, down the stairs, until I was outside again.

Punching up the police station's address in my phone, I began to follow the map like Frodo trudging toward Mount Doom, but instead of a ring, I was throwing in a revolver. The closer I got to the police station, the more I wanted to run back home.

Olivia held my hand, reminding me she was still there and that she'd lead me to my destination.

Step by step, my fate sealed before my eyes until I was in front of the entrance to the police station.

Glass double doors stood before me. Reaching for the metal bar on the left door, I pushed it open and entered.

Olivia was gone. I had to finish the rest of this journey alone.

An almost empty lobby sprawled out before me with a metal detector about ten yards away with three police officers manning who came in and out of their castle.

No other people were around.

The squeak of my shoes was the only sound in the room as I walked slowly toward the looming door-frame-shaped security detectors and the X-ray conveyor belt platform next to it. I didn't want to be shot on sight pulling out a gun, but I wanted to turn myself in along with the gun, so I took my backpack off my shoulders and readied the Wanted sign of the man who attacked me.

As I arrived at the front of the conveyor belt, the officer with the name tag "T. Cortez" motioned to my bag. "Open your backpack, please."

I was going to puke.

Please don't shoot me. Please don't shoot me.

With shaking hands, I unzipped the backpack, then handed it directly into Officer Cortez's hands.

I placed my hands up in surrender to show them I didn't have anything else on me.

Here I go.

"Officer Cortez, my name is Jeraline Arnold, and I'm here to make a confession. There's a gun in that backpack, and I shot the man in that Wanted poster with it. His blood is on the shirt inside." My voice shook, but I hoped I sounded sane and calm.

Officer Cortez's body tensed at my admission, and he motioned for the other two officers to stand next to me while he examined the interior of my backpack. He carefully pulled out the giant revolver and raised an eyebrow in surprise, then checked the bullet chamber all without comment. Glancing at my attacker's Wanted poster, he showed it to the other two officers, and to my horror, they nodded in what I could only describe as recognition.

"We've been looking for you," Officer Cortez said solemnly.

"I thought so." Time was up.

"Follow me."

Holding back tears, I tried to swallow, but the lump in my throat made it impossible.

Making our way past the metal detector, I followed Officer Cortez into the belly of the police station, which basically was a bunch of cubicles, not as intimidating as I had imagined. Wending past the main area, the officer led me down a hallway with a line of closed doors. Picking one in the middle, he unlocked the door,

179

opened it, and held his hand out for me to enter.

An interrogation room.

Deep breath.

I was expecting this.

One table, two opposing chairs, stark and empty. No two-way mirror though. That was different from every TV show and movie I'd ever seen. Motioning to either chair, Officer Cortez almost looked . . . friendly? I must be imagining things. "Have a seat. I'll be with you in a moment."

I sat down on one of the seats as the officer shut the door behind him, locking me in alone. Okay, I didn't hear him locking the door, but maybe since I turned myself in, I wasn't a flight risk.

Placing my hands on the table, I tried to get them to stop shaking.

Both Edmond Dantès and Hercule Poirot popped in across from me, leaning against the wall.

Poirot spoke first with a nod of approval. "I'm proud of you for turning yourself in."

Edmond sneered in disgust as he eyed Poirot, then turned toward me. "Now you'll be in prison and completely helpless. At least with your freedom you had options."

Poirot huffed. "Looking over her shoulder forever? What kind of life is that?"

Crossing his arms, Edmond said, "The kind where the bad guy got what he deserved and the good guy wins."

I had to stop him. "But shooting him makes me the bad guy."

Edmond scoffed. "That's absurd."

Poirot nodded emphatically. "It's the truth."

Sighing, I answered, "I don't know what it is, but turning

myself in was something I had to do."

Both Poirot and Edmond appeared to concede to this, and they disappeared as Officer Cortez walked into the room with a handful of paperwork. I was sure I was about to be handcuffed, so I placed my hands out in front of me to make it easier on him.

Officer Cortez sat across from me, took an envelope off the top of his paperwork, and slid it over. "Open it," he advised.

"Aren't you going to cuff me?" I wasn't sure what was happening.

Was that a smile? Did he just smile at *me*? A murderer?

I opened the envelope, not sure what to expect, but a check written out to me for a hundred dollars was not on my radar. "What is this?"

"It's a reward for the capture of Alex Peters," he said frankly.

"What?" What?

"A neighbor saw the whole thing. You being attacked, Alex hitting his head and passing out on top of you." Officer Cortez fumbled through the paperwork until he found what he was looking for and slid it over.

A witness statement. Stating exactly what Officer Cortez had told me.

I didn't understand.

"But I shot him," was all that came out.

The officer shook his head, obviously not sure how to respond. "No bullet has been fired from your gun. It's brand new, no residue, and the chamber is empty. I don't think bullets have ever been loaded into it. You didn't shoot anyone."

"But I heard it." What was happening?

Officer Cortez shrugged as if that very shrug solved everything.

"I'm not sure what you heard, but it wasn't a gunshot. Alex was still unconscious by the time we got there, but he's been yapping ever since, claiming you were a six-foot monster that attacked him."

"He's . . . he's okay?" My brain was having trouble processing the information.

"Oh yeah, no concussion. He'll be fine. We've been after him for a while now . . ."

At this point, the officer continued to talk, to explain, to chuckle, but it all became a warbled jumble in my brain. I didn't shoot him. The shot I heard was from my imagination, from my terror, from the part of me that needed to get away, that felt helpless as he tried to hurt me. It all made an alarming kind of sense. Grandma didn't buy any bullets. She just bought the gun, and I didn't know anything about guns other than they shoot and kill people. She had wanted me to take lessons, so of course she'd never hand me a loaded weapon I could accidentally discharge. I was so wrapped up in the sheer and utter terror of being near a gun, I hadn't thought about any of it logically.

Officer Cortez's voice slowly faded back in as my thoughts began to clear. "So there's your reward. We'll need your statement as well, and I'm assuming you'll be pressing charges. Did you want your weapon back?"

"No. You keep it. I don't want it anymore." And that was the truth.

Officer Cortez seemed to be taking in my frazzled state because he nodded, his expression gentle. "Probably for the best." He slid over a small stack of the paperwork along with a pen. "If you could sign those forms, you'll be all set to go."

I read through the paperwork, and the more I read, the lighter I began to feel. This was real. This was happening. My attacker, Alex Peters, was alive, not even injured.

Signing the last piece, I slid it back to the officer. He gathered the paper into a pile, stood, then extended his hand for me to shake. I took it awkwardly, but a part of me wanted to leap across the table and give him a hug.

"Someone will call you if we need you to testify, but honestly, the case against him is as solid as they come. We probably won't need you." He took his hand back and motioned to the reward check with a nod and a wink. "Don't spend it all in one place."

I was dazed, but I managed a smile as he left.

I didn't kill anyone.

I wasn't a murderer.

I was alive.

And I was free.

HAPPY ENDING
(Because, yeah, that's what we all deserve.)

The warmth of the sun hit my face as I walked out of the police station. It had never felt as calming as it did in that moment. I basked in its rays, closing my eyes, letting what had happened truly sink in.

"Excuse me." A woman's voice brought me out of my reverie.

I opened my eyes. Not a good idea to stop and stand still right near the entrance doors. "Oh, sorry." I moved away from the entrance.

But the stranger smiled. "No worries. I wouldn't have said anything if I'd been able to open the door without hitting you. You looked really . . . happy." Without waiting for an answer from me, she entered the building.

Happy.

Yes.

I was . . . happy.

The vibration of my cell phone buzzed in my pants pocket,

and I pulled it out. Not recognizing the number, I answered it anyway. "Hello?"

"Is this Jeraline Arnold?" A cheery woman's voice sounded on the other end.

"Yes." I almost asked it as a question, surely her overenthusiasm had to mean she was a telemarketer.

"I'm from Cassiopeia Design School. I'm calling to tell you that your designs won first prize in our contest!" she practically shrilled with excitement.

Heart drop.

"What?" I squeaked. Yup. I actually squeaked.

"Congratulations! You just earned yourself a full scholarship!" She squeaked too.

There was all sorts of squeaking going on, feeding off of each other's excitement.

"But what about what happened with my dress?" Why did I bring that up? Self-sabotage much?

But her tone went from peppy to sympathetic in an instant as she said, "That was horrible. I'm so sorry that happened to you, but it wasn't your fault." The pep came back full force as she added, "Besides, the modeling is just for show. It's the designs that matter."

"And you like them?"

A genuine, hearty laugh. "We love them! Your ideas are . . . magical. That's the word we all thought of when looking through them."

Magical.

My entire being lit up, and my body flushed with the intensity. "Thank you," I managed to stutter. "Thank you so

185

much." I choked back a cry of joy.

The woman's voice bubbled with happiness. "Listen, come down to our office next Friday, and we'll set everything up, okay?"

I let out a whoop of excitement, not caring if I looked stupid, not caring that the man who walked past me cringed. "I will. Thank you again."

The woman's laugh was what I imagined a twinkling fairy to sound like. "Can't wait to have you at our school. Have a great day, Jeraline."

"You too."

And she hung up.

I won.

I really won.

And I knew exactly what I needed to do. What I wanted to do.

Racing home, I was on a mission.

I threw my bedroom door open, gathered the broken dress still on my floor, and began to sew. I fixed every seam and replaced every bead that had fallen off, until finally I only had one more bead to add, the largest of them all: the star my parents named after me. The place where I knew they waited for me a long, long time from now.

The dress was finished. Complete.

I put it on along with the petticoat, then turned toward the mirror.

It was just as stunning as it had been before I stepped foot on the runway that day. I could admit it without flinching from self-doubt. And I looked stunning too. Because . . . because I was me, and for the first time in a really long time, I found that

I truly liked me.

Picking up the unframed picture of my parents on my bedside table, I hugged it fiercely, then placed it back.

One last hurdle to jump.

Putting on some lipstick, fussing a bit with my hair, I left the apartment.

I arrived at the alley quicker than I expected. Things we fear are often like that. But I had to do this. I had to move forward, and this alley was a part of that.

I had let it become the center of everything I feared in life, and now, as I really looked at it: it was just an alley. A grotesque, dirty and dark alley, but no longer the embodiment of what scared me.

Taking a step forward, my foot disappeared in the darkness.

Maybe I spoke too soon.

I'm not afraid.

I'm not afraid.

I'm not afraid.

Or, I didn't *want* to be afraid.

That felt right.

I took another step forward, and light began to seep in, slowly, but enough that shadowed outlines of fire escapes and dumpsters materialized in front of me instead of the fog of black.

The further I walked in, the brighter it grew, until I heard footsteps and a silhouette of a man coming toward me.

Old instincts crept in, and I almost ran.

Emma appeared next to me though. "You got this," she said with a smile. "Don't be afraid."

And suddenly . . .

I wasn't.

"Jeraline?"

Emma disappeared as the figure turned into Josh, materializing out of the shadows of the alley, his face wracked with worry as he approached. "I've been looking all over for you. I went to your apartment after your phone call, then I went to Buster's . . ." His eyes widened in awe as he truly saw me. "Jeraline . . ."

"I'm okay," I reassured him. "More than okay. I'm better than I've been in a really long time."

Josh brushed his hand against my cheek. "When you said you shot someone . . . I got so scared."

Reaching out, I gently took his hands in mine. "I know. I'm sorry I scared you. But I was wrong. I didn't hurt anyone."

Blood rushed through my veins until the pounding in my heart was overwhelming.

I wasn't a killer.

It was such an intense feeling of relief, my knees wobbled slightly.

Josh caught me, his hands now around my waist. Then he stared at me again, as if each new moment shell-shocked him. "You . . . you're just so beautiful."

My face burned in what I was sure was a full-on blush. "Thank you."

He kept staring, shaking his head in wonderment. "I mean it. You're the most beautiful person I've ever met. I'm the luckiest guy in the world." He looked down, embarrassed. "I mean, I know we only went on one date . . . I didn't mean to assume . . ."

I kissed him.

When I pulled back, his worry had been replaced with a

silly grin. He eyed our surroundings. "We should get out of this creepy place."

"This place isn't creepy. I think it's beautiful." My whole being beamed with a sense of calm and purpose I'd never experienced before. Holding out my arms in a waltzing position, I looked up expectantly at Josh.

"You want to dance *here?*" he asked, watching me with a dazed expression.

I nodded.

Tilting his head to the side with amusement, Josh chuckled. "Well, okay then."

Carefully taking my arms in his, Josh led the dance, and we waltzed among the garbage and the dark as if it were the marble floor of a fairy-tale castle.

Before our eyes, the alley grew lighter and lighter, the sun deciding at that very moment to shine directly in its center.

Our feet left the ground as we floated into the air, oblivious to the world around us.

I knew I had nothing to fear anymore.

Life would still be hard, but I could face it now.

And in that very moment, as Josh's T-shirt and jeans transformed into a double-breasted tuxedo and we danced among the stars of the universe, I could truly be happy.

I could truly be me.

OTHER BOOKS BY BECCA C. SMITH

THE RISER SAGA

Riser
Reaper
Ripper

THE ATLAS SERIES

Atlas
Grigori Returned
The Underworld

RISER & ATLAS FINALE

Atlas Rising

DREAM DIARIES

The Dream Diaries
The Dream Diaries: Blood Ties

THE ALEXIS TAPPENDORF SERIES

Alexis Tappendorf and the Search For Beale's Treasure
Alexis Tappendofr and the Search For Atlantis

LOVE & DARK SERIES (With Hina McCord)

Vessel
First Born
Gutian Code